Bill Allerton lives, sleeps, drinks, writes and worries in his native Sheffield, a place he leaves occasionally on foreign travel to gather experience and images. In his writing, as in life, he claims the ability to walk through doors into emotional and unexpected situations with the same purposeful stride.

Working from a previous platform of narrative poetry, spoken-word recordings and live performances, a play and prize-winning short stories, Bill has a further two novels due for publication mid 2014.

Available Now;

The Train …and Other Tracks
(*A collection of Narrative Poetry and Short Stories available as spoken word on CD or MP3 download direct from the publisher*)

Sir Tingly & The Dargon
(*An engaging story for children of all ages. Available as spoken word on CD or MP3 download direct from the publisher. Text version coming soon for Kindle*)

Email for information to: *cybermousemm@gmail.com*

Also by this author

To Kill a Wish
(*A collection of short fiction*)

A Day for Tigers
(*A collection of short Science Fiction*

Published by Cybermouse MultiMedia Ltd. 2013
101 Cross Lane
Sheffield S10 1WN
Email: cybermousemm@gmail.com

This book is a work of fiction. Names, characters, places and incidents are either a product of the Author's imagination or are used fictitiously.

Cybermouse MultiMedia Ltd.
would like to thank Soren Andersen
for permission to use his father's
outstanding artwork as a cover.

THE FOX AND THE FISH
by Thomas Andersen
(an acrylic painting on canvas
size of original work 61 × 76 cm)

(© Thomas Andersen/billedkunst.dk/ DACS 2013)
www.andersenart.com.au

See more of the Artists work at:
http://www.redbubble.com/people/arttas

The Fox & The Fish

A Cry for Anarchy, Freedom, Love and Immortality

Bill Allerton

To my Lover, Friend and Mentor

Bryony Doran

*Without whose Love, Persistence and Sacrifice
I might never have finished this book.*

Bryony Doran - Author of
'The China Bird' and 'The Sand Eggs'
http://www.bryonydoran.com

I would also like to thank
Andrew Nimmo
*my good friend and the brother I never had,
for his faith in me and his efforts in publishing this novel.*

Chapters:

Cont.:

Crossing The Ruby

'McEarly? Are you drunk?'

…it's The Ruby …priceless and standing over me in all her Friday finery topped off by the dark serge reefer that once was her father's when he worked the Railway…

Only on Promises, I tell her.

'You ever keep them, McEarly?'

Rarely, I say.

'Will you make *me* one?' says the Ruby.

Promises are like coffins, I say, A man puts his foot in one only when he has to.

The Ruby turns away for a moment. Her Mammy is still over the other corner, head lifting as she admires the new paint recently applied to the toilet door and somewhat inadvertently to the sleeve of my best jacket.

The Ruby sits down beside me.

'Explain…' she says.

…and as she licks the last drop of barley wine from her glass with the pinkness of her tip I see at once the small smudge of lipstick on her left canine like the red blood left by the rending of flesh and I want to erase it with the dry roughness of my tongue…

A Promise is forever, I say, just like a coffin… so it behoves a man to make one that fits. Imagine your knees up to your chest and waiting for the Trump of Doom that might not arrive for some while? What would you give for a stretch?

'And here's me thinking you had the sense of it, McEarly.'

Alright, I say, I promise to always remember your hair.

'What if you get the Old Timers disease?' says the Ruby.

…and she leans so close to me I can almost taste the perfume she's rubbed in. I recognise it from sliding around the beauty counters at the department store. It does have a name... but then so do most other things I once cared to remember…

'You better touch it, McEarly.'

…I reach up my hand and watch the tips disappear in a tangle of dark ginger and taste the silk chocolate of it on my skin...

'No,' says the Ruby, and takes hold of my fingers, '…like this.'

She pushes them warm against her scalp …down where the roots are a hack of jungle and the delicate surprise of her ear. I wander in silence and the only wind is the wind of her breath and as I fall closer no barley ever tasted more like wine.

The Ruby leads my hand away, 'Now you'll remember,' she says, '…but that's such a small promise are you sure you can fit into it?'

I'll make you another if you let me take you home.

'McEarly!' she says, 'Whatever has come over you?'

…I want to say it wasn't me …but that sometimes my mind has a manner of speaking …in a manner of speaking…

If I promise to behave myself, can I see you home the night?

'Which night?'

…the Ruby is leaning closer but I still haven't the name for the scent. I think it's the big-chested-little-blonde-girl-with-the-bluest-eyes at the stall by the corner …and the mouth is now so full of scent and hope that words have to claw their way around them…

The night, I say.

'It's Friday,' says the Ruby,'…and the Mammy always stays out late of a Friday.'

…I look for my watch then remember the Landlord has it for the price of the beer. There's a clock over the bar but I can't bring myself to look beyond her hair…

'What time is it?' says the Ruby.

…as I pour like custard over her skin of apple-pie perfection …her eyes the slender, accusing holes my Mammy made to let out the steam…

The Time of my Life, I tell her.

'You're a man of small necessities,' she says, 'So what's this about taking me home?'

I said that?

'You've been burning holes in me all night with them lazy eyes of yours.'

The Mammy in the corner sits bending and dipping …the ripples in her fat neck working from the quartets spitting her teeth …each one of them with my name on…

The Ruby drags my attention away, 'My sister is here to collect her in about half an hour.'

And then?

'And then you can take me home.'

But the Mammy will be there before us.

'And if we time it right, she'll be in bed.'

What will happen if *I* time it right?

'You promised to behave yourself, McEarly,' says the Ruby.

…and I hear the coffin lid shuffle firmly into place…

The Mammy is leaving on the arm of Beryl. Her eyes catch a hold of mine in a way that wrenches them around in my skull. Her smile is the horn God gave to Joshua …and from the ruins of my emotional Jericho I hear the message…

The Ruby sits back into her seat and the old Railway coat slides from her shoulders in a single movement. Underneath is a cardigan of rare Marks and Spencer quality …and underneath the cardigan is a flimsy …I can't think of a better word …and underneath that …she catches me looking…

'Do you have enough for another drink, McEarly?'

The watch should be good for another two pints yet, I say, why?

'Because I think I would like one.'

Thinking is a rare quality, I say, and a facility that shouldn't be wasted on alcohol. Are you sure that after another drink you will still have the same…

'Cheapskate,' says the Ruby.

She waves two fingers at the Landlord and he nods. When I do that he throws me out. What a charm the Ruby must have…

'What are you thinking?' says the Ruby, 'Quick …while you still have the facility.'

I was thinking that I was thinking what a rare charm you have, I say.

'Then at least we're on the same page,' says the Ruby.

Four pints after I came in the door has been moved…

'Come on,' says the Ruby, 'If the Mammy can get through it, I'm sure you can.'

If it saw the Mammy coming it probably got out of the way.

'What are you saying about the Mammy, McEarly?'

Oh…

…she grabs my lapels as we find the door and the softness of the Ruby is upon me and the scents of her hair and apple-pie skin mingling with the creosote and wrought iron from the Railway jacket and I'm swooning and in a moment of swiftly-passing lucidity I know it's old-fashioned but it fits better than a cheap coffin full of promises and all I'm really thinking is that the Mammy is like one of them Supertankers that takes thirteen miles to stop and thirty more to turn around and the tightening of the Ruby's knuckles tells me I was thinking out loud…

…her leg finds the back of my knee and I go down like a sack in the gutter and the water is going in the shirt collar and out the trouser leg and I'd never have believed someone so fragile could be capable of such utter violence …but now her warmth is upon me …and upon the whole of me…

I wrap my arms around her and will not let go.

'McEarly…' she says, soft in my face as the Atlantic rain… 'McEarly! Let go of me this instant!'

Can't you take it as a compliment? I say.

'McEarly, just remember that I'm from Belfast.'

When I asked to take you home I'd been thinking on the lines of two one pound-forties on the number fifty-two, not a thirty-pound taxi fare, I say.

She shakes her head and the hair falls full across my face.

Ruby, I say, just hold your gob still while I kiss it.

'And why would you want to kiss it.'

Because…

…because you have some lipstick on a tooth that's driving me mad unless I can lick it off…

I feel her collapse against me. I slacken my arms and suddenly she's grabbing me and punching.

Was that a feint? I say.

…for you never know when the use of a good vocabulary might be appreciated…

I feel her shaking against me as we roll from the gutter, winkling out each other's senses with sharp sticks of laughter in the spillings of the rain.

'So the Mammy's a tanker, is she?'

She beats me gently around the head. I grab her wrists as John Donald's boy strides over us.

'Hang on in there, Julius,' he says, 'I've seen the arse of her. It has the hand of Harland and Wolff all over it.'

…and as he strides there is a hole in the sole of his left shoe and a sticker from the charity shop in the arch of the right and I want him to come back so I can see how much he paid but now he's gone and there's just me and the Ruby and she is laughing …against my chest …inside my shirt …her head thrown back and her throat open wide …whooshing the night air with tones from the wonderful organ insides of her.

'*Julius*,' says the Ruby, and collapses again.

The bus driver makes me stand the whole way and will not reduce the fare.

The rain comes on again the moment we step from the bus. We're under a new shelter but someone has stolen the curved glass roof panels. The Ruby has the collar up on the reefer and it sheds water from the creosote to go in through the warp and weft of me until I'm soaked back and front. I look down and I'm sure I can see another inch of shoe.

'What you looking at, McEarly?' says the Ruby.

I think I'm getting taller by the minute.

'Alright then, Big Man. That's my house by the dog bin.'

Location is everything …but I thought it was the Mammy's house? I say

'She gave it me years ago so the Council couldn't have it for the caring money. Thought it might attract a man for me.'

She looks up into my eyes and I see the rain leaking from the corners of hers…

'I shouldn't have said that, McEarly, you'll think me desperate. But I'm not …I've just been saving it.'

Her smile folds against the tweed of my Friday jacket where I hope she doesn't mind a touch of the lemon yellow paint. My nose is in the scented forest of her hair and doesn't want to find the way out. Thursday lunch I'll go down the store and when I find it I'll buy her some.

'I'm sorry I laughed,' says the Ruby.

Around us, moths are zapping the street lamp like a film run slow and every wing beat is a heartbeat I feel through the tweed and the shirt and the small patch of curls on the chest I never comb in front of the mirror.

What?

'I'm sorry I laughed,' she says.

It was nothing, I say.

'That's what I'd heard,' says the Ruby, 'But it wasn't.'

It wasn't what?

'It wasn't a nothing.'

So was it Kant or Confucius who said that if a something wasn't a nothing... then it must be a something?

'No, McEarly, it was the Mammy.'

And what would the Mammy know about my appendant particles?

'She said that by the look of you they would be something and nothing.'

And? I say.

'And it was ...something. Alright? And you can stop smirking, McEarly.' The Ruby reaches up to pull down the corners of my mouth, 'It wasn't that much of a something.'

'The bus...' she says.

...but my hands have found their way inside her coat where the paint will only rub off on the lining and not show and the fingers of them trawling the lace of her cardigan like caught fish too small to keep until I'm touching the flimsy with my skin...

The bus roars to the stop and the door shishes open. The driver shouts, 'Are ye getting on, McEarly?'

...and I want to tell him to wait because I'm a shimmering fish leaping through this wonderful mouth that has just the now reached up to fill mine with a kiss. Her tongue is snaking over and around the teeth and I recoil so I can see her eyes and they are smiling...

Ruby ...I ...

'Save it, McEarly,' says the Ruby, 'It will keep to the next Friday.'

'Are ye getting on, McEarly?' says the driver, 'You're making me late.'

...and he has the head start on me with his creased trousers and brown-stained fingers that run the sawmill of twenty Benson and Hedges between every Terminus...

The Ruby detaches herself and looks up to the bedroom window that burns in the brickwork like a reproachful eye.

'Goodnight, McEarly. I can't let you in this time ...but you kept your promise,' she says.

I stand with one foot on the step of the bus and one by the dog bin and watch her walk the walk.

'McEarly!' says the driver and shishes the door. It bounces open again for my arm is still inside the bus grabbing the rail to keep me from swimming along her path. I lose sight of the Ruby. A light winks on behind the frosted glass panel and I see the Railway coat hung on a frosted glass hook.

Take me away, I mumble.

'What was that?' says the driver.

I'm a fish.

'What?'

I said ...I'm a *Fish*!

'Well ...it is the Friday,' he says.

I press the buzzer.

'What you doing, McEarly. You don't live here.'

I look down and there's a smudge of paint on the bus leather and he won't find it until his next cigarette and by then I'll be gone.

I feel sick, I tell him, and your own doorstep is not the best place.

'I blame it on the dog, myself.'

I don't have a dog.

…and now the bus is turning the last corner and the beer is a recurring warmth in my throat where the acid will find its way home tomorrow like a painfully neutered cat…

'It's me that has the dog, McEarly,' he says, 'A Jack Russell. Do you know them?'

…and me with the mark of the strong little legs fresh on the shin from the day I looked after Sheary's while his wife was up the hospital. I dropped a chicken straight from the oven and he was on it before it hit the floor. I never gave such a howl of satisfaction myself …not even with Kayla Shaughnessy who is ruinously good and coinously available to anyone wearing bicycle clips…

Does the wife not take it to the veterinary? I say.

'I tell her it's because of the Friday that I feed him the sardines.'

It's a very convenient fish, I say, but I prefer the Cod. I have such a reclusive one I have spent all the night trying to find a warm place for it to hide.

'You were never going in with the Mammy there, McEarly,' he says, 'Buy yourself a dog.'

I'm sat over the wheel arch and there's a tick under my arse like a nail in the tyre or my heart stuck to the outside of the rubber like the sticker on John Donald's boy's shoe. The universe yawns and streetlights blend moiré patterns around the rain spots of the window.

I'll stick with the fish, thank you.

The moon is running a ladder up the sky with only the half showing from under her skirts. I stare out at the gutters cleansed of Ruby and the lipstick that I forgot to lick… but life is nothing if not a catalogue of missed opportunity and offers from IKEA.

'Do you *like* fish?' says the driver.

I *am* a fish.

'Would you like a sardine?' he says.

He's out of the cab and opening his snap tin …fingers unearthing white bread smeared with the blood of tomato-christened slivers.

'The dog won't eat them,' he tells me.

You think the wife doesn't notice?

'It's symptomatic.'

I'm not keen on the music, I say, It's a possible hole in my life.

He offers a sandwich across the aisle.

What do you think I am …a cannibal?

'Sit your arse down, McEarly. The rain is up at the window and I want to talk to you.'

I lean back and the moon has drawn her elegantly predictable skirts above a cloud.

'Why won't you consider the dog, McEarly?'

His teeth are red in the soft bones of the fish. Arteries of tomato sauce overlap the colour of old vines streaking his skin.

Are you trying to sell me your dog?

'No, McEarly. If I did that I'd have to get off the two stops before like you. I'm trying to sell you the *idea*.'

There is a fleck of sardine swimming the crease of his lips and when he gets home not even the dog will want to lick it off.

'If you buy a dog,' he says, 'You don't need a relationship.'

I'd sooner have the Ruby.

'You can have the both,' he says.

I'd sooner have the Ruby.

'No,' he says, 'If it's affection you want …buy a Jack Russell.'

Curled up in the bus shelter under a greatcoat is Sheary. I touch his shoulder.

Sheary, I say, Is it the wife? You're two streets away. This can't be you…

'*Why don't you just feck off,*' he says.

So I do.

I cross the street and walk the fifty yards to the first junction. By the corner is Sheary's dog with the print of a bus tyre the length of it like it was still running and the metal disk missing from the collar.

I hear the skitter of a Night-Fox circling beyond the pools of lamplight …in a dark world where nothing goes to waste.

Occam's Safety Razor

'Space and Time are bent,' says Dealy.

I thought the EU straightened all that out …along with the cucumbers.

'The only question that remains,' he says, '…is just how bent it is …and that was bananas.'

Dealy is standing in the timberyard over the tea grate where the swills are poured …the Lardy Cake in his hand describing ellipses of which Kepler would have been calculatingly proud…

'You think you're looking straight at the world…' he says.

His eyes squint up somewhere in the back of his head and the Lardy Cake launches into an exponential curve that shatters a hundred dimensions without spilling the least bit of crumb.

'…but you're not.'

The world has never looked straight at me …with its unexpected lemon-yellows and reluctance of warm places to fettle a cod …so why should I care?

'When you set off to the bar of a Friday,' says Dealy, '…you think it's a straight line …don't you?'

It never is on the way back, I say, Perhaps you have a higher level of expectation than myself.

'No,' says Dealy, 'I'm talking here about a hypothetical straight line.'

Then why didn't you say in the first place?

'But it isn't straight,' he says, 'It's a curve described by a Localised Gravitational Mass.'

Isn't that the one held mid-week just after Easter?

'You're not trying to take this seriously,' says Dealy.

I assure him I am…

'You think you're so high and *feck'n* mighty with your two across and four down in eleven letters and the third one is 'f'.'

'Influential', I tell him.

'I had the jab,' he says, 'and no *feck'n* wonder they won't let you in the cabin to do the crossword. You can't even count for there's only the nine.'

There is no straight line between Dealy's house and the bar. I remind him of that.

'This is designed to perpetuate the Illusion of Normality,' he says, 'They think that if nothing has a straight line you won't notice.'

So who's in on this Conspiracy?

'Everybody who *is* Anybody.'

The Council?

The Lardy Cake is down by the half now …a serried arc just short of the fingers.

'Everybody.'

Even me?

'Don't be *feck'n* stupid,' he says, 'You're a *feck'n Nobody.*'

And being a *feck'n Nobody* is the Occam's Razor of Dealy's Multiple Dimension Theory …for whichever I set foot in I'm the *feck'n Nobody* who's known to sit next to the cleverest man on the bus who does the crossword complete each morning.

King of The Ocean

The Landlord holds out a hand for the watch but I wave the wallet at him. Inside is folding money that melts amongst the fingers like butter once you change it.

'You won the Lottery, McEarly?' he says.

I smile behind the parting of the lips. His brother will have told him about me subbing the Holiday Pay …and I don't care …for I have a Date with the Ruby.

The Mammy is in her usual seat by the toilet door …pecking beer and rumbling with old catechism …and I jump when a hand slides the inside of my jacket from behind.

The wallet's not there, I say, it's in the trousers. Just don't hurt me.

And a voice says in my ear, 'Put down your glass and walk quietly out of the pub.'

…I can do this. It's like being told to *feck off* …only with company…

The Ruby spins me on the pavement with a smile I have dreamed of all week amongst a jetsam of coffins.

'We have a Date,' she says, 'Why were you watching the Mammy?'

The Ruby has on a short jacket and no cardigan.

Have you no coat? I ask.

'I'm soaking it to get the paint out,' she says, 'Anyway …it's too hot to wear for the Cinema.'

What's on?

'Lassie Come Home,' she says, 'It's a remake.'

Is it the one we have to take a bus to?

'No,' she says, 'That's closed for repainting after the fire. It's the one by the department store. It's not far.'

No, it isn't.

…I sheltered in the foyer there half the Thursday lunchtime between being thrown out for sniffing the girls…

The Ruby will not sit on the back row. 'You have the reputation,' she says.

I breathe in the heady essence of her hair and sit up.

You changed your perfume.

'That was an old one of the Mammy's. I bought a new one for our Date. Don't you like it?'

…of course I do. …and it's so much nicer than the one for which I nearly had to sign the sex-offenders register…

It's on you, isn't it?

'McEarly, you can be so…'

Symptomatic, I say.

…and she's quiet for a moment …because that's when the lights go down.

I cry my way through the picture and when the dog breaks its leg, oh, how the sardines flow my eyes to swim and shiver in the shifting beams streaking above our heads until I can't help but believe in the reality of it all.

'McEarly,' says the Ruby, 'Look at you. You're a jelly.'

No, I'm not, I say, I'm a Proper Fish.

'And a queer one at that. What kind of a fish?'

A Capital Letter Fish, I say, A Noun Fish.

'Are you the Whale then, McEarly?'

No, I'm a Cod, I say.

…crisp with the batter to slip between your teeth until I'm swimming the blood of you …and the sweet vinegar smell holding on your breath until I'm gone…

'Are you not taking the bus home, McEarly?'
I'm not a sardine, I say.
'I know that, McEarly,' says the Ruby, 'You're a bigger fish altogether.'
Here, I say, reaching into the jacket, I have a present for the Mammy.
Inside the box is a bottle that moonlight beats into a far smaller shape than I had hoped.
She sniffs.
'Oh …McEarly…'
…and the sardines slip her eyes without even the broken leg of a dog to assist them …smudging her lapel with their eyes of mascara black and the silver scales stolen swiftly by the moon…
'Next Friday…' she says.
I can't wait that long.
'I can't either,' says the Ruby, 'But I don't know how I'll keep the Mammy occupied.'
…I could recommend a Jack Russell …but I promised myself to be careful in case I die of over-enthusiasm…
'I'll see you tomorrow at the bar,' says the Ruby.
I set off at strength, leaving the dark reach of the sea behind at great speed …my fins in their shiny new boots splash powerful against the night and I shimmer the gutters and shame the moon with her lifted skirts while above me, cloud propellers churn the starlight …and I stop to watch until the trawl catches me and I'm swept away…
…because I'm King of the Ocean
…Everyman's Friday Night Special
…and I don't care
…because the net around me is pure Ruby.

The God Particle

At some base level it will be found that the Higgs Boson is a rare form of cheese, says Dealy.

…and lacking the Formality of an Education he reserves the right to self-determine where the Truth lies until it leaps up and smacks him wrong…

But when you break the cheese, I tell him, there are always crumbs …so how can cheese be a fundamental particle?

'Crumbs are Fundamental to the Principle of Life,' he says, 'Just ask the birds in my garden.'

So your bicycle is cheese.

'Indubitably,' he says.

Then how do you ride it?

'I don't. I ride the wife's.'

The wife's has no crossbar, I say.

'And mine has nothing at all. Since the lawsuit from the Cinema I had to pawn everything.'

You couldn't have eaten it and staved off the court starvations?

'It was no longer any use at all,' he says, 'I was lucky to get the fifty pence for it. It might as well have been cheese.'

Could you not have painted it with the bitumen and said it belonged to the Tinkers?

'I had none left after painting the Fire Curtain.'

...and I'm trussed by a nostalgia for yellowing adverts of shut-down-shops and rattling Taxis that used to leap out before the slither of the kaleidoscopic beams began ...and I think again of the Ruby and the back row of empty seats ...and ponder the inconsistency of thought that springs to the mind of women in a state of Cinematic distress...

Did you not consider the bitumen inappropriate at the time?

'I was just trying to make it real.'

Then why didn't you paint it with the cheese? I say, At least when it burned we could've enjoyed the smell.

'Are you taking the piss?' says Dealy, 'You're not one of these Fundamental Atheists?'

Oh... no, no, no. I firmly believe that cheese is the God's Particle. ...except for the one Cheddar with live chillies...

'But you refuse to believe that the Universe is pure Gruyere.'

...this is becoming a little heavy for the Monday lunchtime ...littered as we are between us with the remains of chipboard and glue infiltrating our sandwiches...

It does run true as a Swiss clock, I say.

'No,' he says, 'You lack the gist of it. The Universe is in the holes.'

But in the holes there is nothing...

'The holes are a gaseous excrescence of Multiverse Dimensions', he says, 'Eternally expanding into the consciousness of the cheese between.'

Can you not get the Foreman to take you off the gluepot?

'By the way,' he says, menacing with a Lardy Cake in his hand, 'I know it was you told Kayla Shaughnessy.'

Told her what?

'That the bicycle clips belonged to my wife.'

It wasn't me, I lie, It was some other Idiot.

The Lardy Cake spits particles of pork fat to spin and whirl the air.

'And there's only one of them around here,' says Dealy.

That's saved you an awful lot of money, I say, It'll help cope with the inflation.

'Since when did Fundamental Atheists understand the Principle of Inflation?' he says.

…in about five minutes, I reckon…

'The Principle is this…'

…it's Monday and he's unstoppable. His jobs on the fiddle have dried since the Cinema debacle and there's so much residual energy striding within the man that it takes more than the gluepot to account for it…

'…if something has twenty slices and then it gets bigger… so do the slices. This is your basic Theory of Relativity right here and now.'

So Energy = Mature Cheddar squares?

'Exactly. So there's only so much flour in a cake …and the more you let it rise the bigger it gets …so although the slices look bigger there's only relatively the same amount of Matter in each one.'

…like the little cake my Mammy baked ready and tinned up for her very own Wake and thirty-four turned up …I hate to point this out as a Fatal Flaw so I take a firm grip on the Idiot and accept the Fundamentalist contention…

The same amount of Cheese, I say.

'No,' says Dealy, 'Cheesecake is different.'

Was Einstein fat? I ask.

'No,' says Dealy, 'Being the Jewish he wouldn't have had the Lardy Cake.'

Then what did he have for inspiration?

'The Cheese,' says Dealy.

…and in his eyes there is the gleam of finality for which I have patiently waited…

'But since the Universe has Inflation it now costs more and the wife will not put it in the sandwiches.'

She's a Fundamentally Prudent Woman, I remark.

'Next time you visit the bathroom…' says Dealy, '…examine yourself. You'll find cheese in the most Fundamental of places.'

Is that how Einstein found it?

'No.' says Dealy, 'I told you. He was the Jewish.'

Sheary is a teatime shuffle along a wet street with constant glances behind for the jingle of a collar the bus shrugged into the night somewhere between last week and forever. By morning the foxes had dragged the dog whole and digestible back to earth. Despite his passion for the recycling Sheary will never get over it …and the look of missing attention is set so deep within his eyes it would be a misfortune to catch the glimpse…

Sheary, I nod.

'*Why don't you…*'

Sheary, I say …and catch his arm as he passes, Were you a Mammy in another life?

'God, McEarly …Don't tell me there's another one.'

…in another life I was Julius McEarly …but now I'm a Fish…

I look him up and down.

I don't think you need to worry, I tell him, You're a Fundamental Particle.

'…*feck off.*' he says.

I walk back the way he came …and all I can smell is cheese.

Strawberries in The Dark

The Ruby's hair is finely fettled and gets me a smack on the hand when I try to touch it.

'So,' she says, '…where are you taking me?'

…now there's a thought I hadn't had…

Cinema?

'We went last week …and anyway they're still repainting.'

The park?

The Ruby's eye lifts, 'It'll be dark soon.'

…now there was a thought I *had* had…

The Ruby takes my hand and runs her fingers across it, examining the knuckles for whiskers …but there's still only three-quarters of the moon.

'Do you have no hairs at all, McEarly?'

Are you for the exploring? I ask her.

…and if I let you touch them will you fill your coffin with a promise to remember…

'Are you in front of yourself, McEarly?' says the Ruby.

…only in the morning mirror with the sharp teeth of my little comb and the thin legs and knobbly joints and the face turning autumn with the stubble of it…

The Ruby catches my sleeve to drag me away from her looking-glass eyes. There is a paper bag roll-topped in her fingers.

What have you there? I ask.

'Strawberries,' says the Ruby.

Aren't they a bit late?

'Beryl has a new cloche.'

A park is one of the few places that remained where I left them on the day I exited childhood. I feel betrayed by any changes but aware that parks could feel the same about me if pushed.

The river is deepest under the bridge …like the one where I risked the sure and certain Tetanus Death to swim and never caught it because unknown to me I was a codling with the immunity of scales. The water shivers with reflection as I hang memories like rusty lover's locks along this alien balustrade.

'What are you thinking?' asks the Ruby beside me.

…I never think so I'm not sure how to reply …it's more a process of mind-time unravelling …like the decay of Dealy's Universal Cheese into entropic chaos through the auspices of a particular brightly-coloured mould…

Time is blue, I say.

We walk for a while uncertain of direction until the light is almost gone and the grass is grey as twilight in the yellow glare from the road above.

'Never had you for a silent man, McEarly.'

Sometimes I'm a little self-absorbed, I say.

'Like blotting paper,' says the Ruby.

The moon is up now. Her skirt is above the ankles and the trees comb her light into fine strands of witching-hair that fix the path like the curl of my chest where the laughter of the Ruby is fast imprinted …and when I wake it in the night with my fingers it shows never a sign of the wane.

The darkness of ancient oak folds moth-wings around us while I search her mouth for the taste of the lipstick on the tooth …which I am too late to find.

The Ruby pulls away, 'What are you doing, McEarly? Not that it isn't interesting...'

I search the darkness for her mouth to stop it from asking questions.

My hands are inside her Da's coat and I'm hyperventilating because her lungs are attached to mine and we are the one animal locked into a cycle of hypoxia ...and hallucination is kicking in because under my hands I feel the skin of her and they're moving and God-willing this is real and I'm behind her fire curtain melting away in hooks and nets and the slide of seeking fish until I'm pushed away ...gills pumping in indecent haste ...seduced by a Ruby poacher's light over the gunwale and hoisted clear of the water...

Behind my closed eyes are the twin yellow suns of oxygen starvation.

'Is there something you should ask me first?' the Ruby says.

Do you ever get offers from IKEA? I say.

The Ruby throws her arms around my neck.

'You say the most romantic things,' she says, 'You're right. We could furnish your flat and the Mammy can have it.'

Have you seen my flat?

...my flat is elegant proof of Dealy's hypothesis ...an expanding excrescence of Multi-Dimensional Fundamental Particles ...but without gas. The landlord turned off the meter because he was convinced I was robbing it. What use would there be in robbing it? Between the bar and Kayla Shaughnessy there was never enough coin left to drop one in...

'Not yet...' says the Ruby.

I would need notice.

...and perhaps a week off from work ...and now the reefer is being buttoned up solid and the hands are smoothing the cloth and the smile is becoming rigid...

'I'm not a woman for imprinting with the tree bark,' says the Ruby, 'Or the stains from the grass. So there's your notice.'

'The flat isn't as bad as I expected,' says the Ruby.

I think her comment is over the bar of my expectation, too.

'This bit's quite clean.'

I look around for somewhere that doesn't have a layer of paper preventing the dust from settling the surfaces. Which bit?

'Here…' she says.

Where?

'You can't see it,' says the Ruby.

And why not?

…have we slipped into a Dealy Dimension here or is this the normal one where Confusion reigns Supreme…?

'Because I'm stood on it,' she says.

Where?

'McEarly …it's like to be under my feet. Is it not?'

Then how can I see it?

'You'll have to take my word for it,' she says.

I stare around the flat and sure as it's Christmas her word is the only thing left of any value.

The Ruby turns around and opens a door behind her.

'That explains it, McEarly.'

An explicable corner of the Universe?

'No, McEarly. It's the cupboard in which you keep the hoover.'

It's unusable, I tell her, It fails to differentiate between paper and dust. They should come with more instruction …lessons maybe.

'Like the car?'

…how does the Ruby know about the car? In a moment of pure terror I wonder if she means the one for which I was geographically challenged or the one for the physiologically impossible posturing…

'Why does your face twist up like that, McEarly?'

It's the pain, I say.

…I was trying not to remember the physiological posturing but the leg cramped up again and the Ruby doesn't need to know about that…

'If it's what I think you're thinking, McEarly, I'm not the girl for doing things on a pile of old papers.'

…Papers …Tree bark …Grass Stains …What kind of a world is it coming to when natural discomforts outweigh the shared nestling of oils and fresh salt scents …and the imagining of the slither-slide between us is becoming a growing comfort to know…

'McEarly …you're sweating.'

…profusely …as rivulet as Dealy's drivel of a morning break …and each drop as salt as the ocean in which I had lately thought myself King…

It's hot in here?

'Only under your collar,' says the Ruby, 'Put it away, McEarly.'

I look down to where my appendant particles remain suitably sheathed by the trousers.

'Not that, McEarly…'

I look up into her eyes and sure the Mammy's are staring back at me.

'…the very thought of it.' she says.

Why Buy When You Can Rent

Kayla Shaughnessy is in the process of exiting Sheary's door in a backwards direction. In her hands is a white box she acquired from the War Surplus shop. It has a red cross upon it and once strapped to the side of an ambulance had seen service from Killybareen to Khartoum and though no money had changed hands, Reardon says his one regret was that he hadn't asked for instalments.

Nurse Shaughnessy, I presume.

'God, McEarly. You make me sound like Doctor Livingstone.'

…she forgets …I too have been lost in the intimacy of her jungle…

Is Sheary ill? I ask.

She puts the box down to smooth her apron. 'Patient Confidentiality,' she says.

If you can pretend to be the nurse, I say, the least you can do is pretend to give me the diagnosis.

'That's easy,' she says, 'You have the look of a man that's not getting any.'

It's the IKEA principle, I say, You start at the front in all the things you don't want and by the time you get to the things you do want there's a blankness of slips and betting-shop pens before the lack of money comes over you.

'I seen you out with that little Connor girl.'

Shaughnessy bends to put the box on the back seat of her car and she's built like a radio that has an amplitude dial.

She turns as she closes the door to make sure I'm still looking.

'McEarly,' she says, 'Why buy when you can rent?'

I'm in the middle of the street and so is the fifty-two bus. From the back it has the girth of the Mammy but a sight better looking and is wedged firmly between two rows of parked cars. The door is shished open at the front and I creep slowly along the green and cream slab of it in case there are sardines rampant …but the cab is empty.

I slither on the platform and think to rush the stair to take the free ride into town but outside the front window is the driver with his back to me and hands on his hips like Miss Lunacy's teapot dance from the Primary School. In front of him is a caravan. It has chromium on its chromium and is so big it has four wheels …presumably on each side but that might be compulsory only under law …and in front of that is the scabbiest lorry I have seen short of the one they found while dredging the reservoir …and in front of that is the world's scabbiest tinker …Jonjo Benigglety of the Viking Ancestor who would have had to put him in the stern to stop the boat pitching to the side …and whose face bears angry tufts of ginger where the razor skips …and a voice says…

'Hello, McEarly. What are you hiding from?'

I look up from my Neanderthal slump behind the bus window and the freshest child's face is staring at me with eyes blacker than I ever saw on a kipper.

You have the wrong man, I say, I'm not McEarly.

'Yes you are,' she says.

…and there are streaks of ingrain beneath the incandescent hair that cascades across her face. A quick glance at the window shows the rest of Benigglety's brood skittering gardens for scrap and tugging door handles and peering all the while through glass with that special Tinker insight…

Are you sure? I ask, because some days I might not be myself.

Her teeth are bright-rooted in a grime-smecked grin and I sense she's laughing at me.

'Your flat is on my patch.'

What are you? I ask.

…because her skin slides as I watch and she's shifting temporal universes the way cats do when they're out hunting the spare milk…

'I'm Feral,' she says.

I ask if she knows what Jack Russell tastes like but she shakes her head and it seems to gather particles from the air around us and I wonder if this is a fundamental property of Tinker hair.

Are you the Fox? I ask.

'Urban,' she says.

Is it you makes that awful scream in the night?

'Give me another five years,' she says.

We're kneeling under the windows on the platform of the bus with hard rubber under us like bark ridges on the Ruby's coat and I venture the question even though I have the inkling of an answer.

What are *you* hiding from?

'I'm not. I'm robbing the bus,' she whispers.

…and no more a flicker of remorse than in the eyes of the kipper …just this lost smokiness that girls practice…

I look around and the bus is empty as far as I can see.

There's no-one in, I say.

'My da' says that's the best time.'

I think he meant houses not buses.

A brush of ginger hair in and out of the small cabin …a rash as coins leave the till. 'How much do they charge you for the fare?'

One pound and sixty pence.

'It's one pound and twenty pence from here to the Mill. Don't be greedy, McEarly.'

Coins slither into my hand.

'Have a week on the council,' she says.

My hand won't go into my pocket. The cloth is shrunk with a Stricture of Honesty and I'm left bemused.

She looms into my eyes, 'Are you *in* today, McEarly?'

Well …no …I'm here and trying to get to work.

'I'll get to you later, then,' she says, 'I'll check my diary.'

There's nothing in the meter.

'I know,' she says.

Dealy has the gluepot warmed through by the time I walk in.

'Did you ever see Sheary?' he says, 'Now there's a poor unfortunate…'

Sheary, I tell him, is a prime example of the Oscar Wilde syndrome.

Dealy's eyes spring empty-wide as cold mash can lids.

'He bats for the other team?'

No, I say, he is the author of his own misfortune.

'We all have a Write to Life,' says Dealy …punctuating Capital Lardy-Cake-Letters.

It's not the writing, I tell him, It's the medical and the partaking of that's his problem.

'Aahh!' says Dealy… 'No…'

Who was the oldest? Sheary or his wife?

'It must be his wife,' says Dealy, 'She died the first. With all decency that's the right thing to do.'

And what happens to a woman when she turns sixty?

'Wouldn't know,' says Dealy, 'I stop looking when they get to forty-eight.'

Why forty-eight?

'Am I not to be allowed a little abstraction?' he says.

When she turns sixty she gets the Pension, I tell him.

'There had to be a reason he kept her around,' says Dealy, 'I thought perhaps the fire might have been better fettled than the mantelpiece.'

And when she gets the Pension?

'A man can go the part-time,' says Dealy.

She gets the Free Prescriptions, I tell him, and because she was rarely ill they used to swap symptoms.

'Whatever they were giving her she didn't look good on it. I'd sooner pay so you know which side of the counter it's from.'

She was so busy with Sheary's symptoms, I say, they took her in for the gall bladder when what she needed was the hysterectomy.

'That's tragic,' says Dealy, 'To think he never got the operation himself. Why do we pay the taxes …and where does a man get the Marital Sympathy required once his wife has up and died? With a gall bladder the like of that he'll never find another.'

Don't worry about Sheary, I say, he's Renting.

Dog Watch

'McEarly?'

...it's the Landlord's brother ...and he's prodding the air with his demon's fork of a right hand and trying to get the attention of which I am jealous and do not give up easily ...it's a source of wonder how so much money can stick to so few fingers ...especially when it's mine.

I don't get paid until tomorrow, I tell him.

'McEarly,' he says, 'You're wanted at the gate.'

...it's the Garda for sure. The money from the bus must be marked and though it wouldn't fit the jacket with the mind of its own the trousers accepted it without question leaving me to consider how fickle eighty percent polyester with twenty percent cotton can be ...and if it had more of the natural fibre I might still be an honest man...

I shuffle the change into a drawer.

Waiting inside the gate is Jonjo Benigglety with the biggest, hardest crush of hands this side of hydraulics.

'McEarly,' he says, 'Can I buy you a pint?'

I can't afford it.

'You don't need the money,' says Benigglety.

...I hadn't meant the money ...I check the watch but it doesn't appear again until tomorrow evening...

It's a bit early, I say, Circular saws and alcohol being something of a mismatch.

Let no-one tell you that a Tinker takes an uneducated perspective on life ...for Benigglety pulls back his sleeve and there are four watches on the wrist including the one Sheary lost over six weeks ago. He takes an average and slides back the cloth.

'It's daylight isn't it?'

...and the inevitable result of drink that much harder to accept unless you've stepped out into the night's confessional and been forgiven by the moon...

It's not yet over the yardarm, I tell him.

'Who isn't?' says Benigglety.

...for a Viking I find him surprisingly nautically unacquainted ...I want to tell him to take his four watches and *feck off* but even I have the survival instinct where it matters...

A bar is a strange place between the hours of four and six with daylight fringing the edge of doors and the steady seep of it between adverts pasted to the inside of the glass.

The Landlord is watching Benigglety for signs of violence of which he is appropriate at any and all states of the tide. He catches my eye then leers at my watch on his wrist in an unwarrantedly lascivious manner.

Come the morrow...

If it's about the bus money, I say, you can have it all back... Thursday.

'You're obliged to keep hold of that,' says Benigglety, 'for Shel says it's your rebate on the electric.'

Shell? Isn't that the petrol rich people put in their little cars?

'My daughter,' says Benigglety, 'It's short. But she's only eleven.'

Perhaps the name will grow along with her.

'It's short for Shelelagh.'

…and I'm right …by the time she's sixteen and begins that awful whooping noise in the night …it will fit exactly…

Benigglety is quiet for a moment while pulling at his beer.

I never touched her, I say.

'I know you didn't,' he says, 'There's a mirror over the bus doorway and I was watching you the while. But you didn't smack her, either.'

Should I have?

'Everyone else does,' says Benigglety, 'Never has a child been so remarkably chastised as that one.'

The Landlord has his hands under the counter gripping hard at the tray of his cash register and I take to thinking about a tinker's communal way of life where chastisement should be shared around in a more equitable manner …and if you could quantify it …how little the taxman would ever see.

She sounds remarkably bright on it.

'I educated her myself,' says Benigglety.

Is that where this chastisement has its stem?

'It's more to do with the death of her mother,' he says.

…I'd never seen Mrs Benigglety …and now I understand why. By the size of her brood I'd imagined her pinned inside a swaying caravan shaved and spread with cervix in a constant state of dilation …and though it sounds so underwhelming in the slow creep of daylight across the dark swill floor I say I'm sorry anyway in the hope that she hadn't suffered…

'Childbirth.' he says, 'So at least she wasn't to suffer the pain of the upbringing. I need the help with Shel.'

I look around to see who else might have come in but the slice of impending light is moving inexorably in my direction with no-one else to bar it.

From me?

'Not just you,' says Benigglety, 'The wife also.'

The chair has sprung rivets. I try to shuffle but fixed as I am by the stern plate I can only await the reconfiguration of Dealy's Dimensionality.

Was it in the paper? I say.

'Was what?' says Benigglety.

The wedding. Was it casual or top hat?

'Surely you remember your own wedding, man?'

...I look around for something else that might have been dislodged by the Universal Shift. The Landlord still grips his cash tray ...still has my watch ...still has the wispy hair that combs over the whole way until someone opens the door when he isn't expecting it ...beer is still expensive and I can't find any advantage to this Dimension at all...

In my other Dimension, I say, I do not have the pleasure of a wife.

'What other Dimension?' says Benigglety.

Perhaps it's Dealy you should be talking to, I say, My Physics Degree arrived inside a box of Cheerios in a little cellophane packet.

'I seen you with her,' says Benigglety, 'Are you saying I don't know what I'm seeing?'

Were you looking through the glass?

'Through the window of the truck,' he says.

Then I won't dispute it.

'I never saw such loving restraint in the way you punched each other,' says Benigglety, 'I knew right that moment you were my man. And when you threw yourself out of kindness into the gutter beneath her ...well.'

That wasn't the wife, I say, just a misunderstanding.

'For sure it was the wife,' says Benigglety, 'In God's name why else would you fight a woman in the street?'

Cabin Fever

'Welcome Home, McEarly.'

Sarcasm becomes you, I say, Have you ever thought of doing it as a stand-up?

…and the Foreman shifts his fat arse on the seat from which it is reluctant to leave between the hours of eight and five and I wonder does he moor it like a scow to the settee for the weekend…

'Work might become you, McEarly.' he says, 'Have you ever thought of trying it?'

It seems an awful trouble for such a small amount of money.

'Speaking of which,' he says, 'I was offered just yesterday the awful amount of money.'

…and I know from experience that his awful amount will not exceed the boundaries of a ten pound note…

'It seems you're valuable, McEarly.'

That's good. I haven't worked three years for nothing then …only almost.

'You had a caller,' he says, 'A Proper Gentleman in Orange Tweed. Wanted to speak to you.'

I'm not for the speaking-to this week.

…only for the inevitable sniping-at over unforeseen absences that mean the watch will have to remain without me until the end of the month…

'He wanted to know where you live.'

That's Personal Information, I say.

...and of course he didn't tell him ...but his eyes are agleam like the strip in a bank note and I'm minded to remind him of the Data Protection Act ...though it will not cover the stamp card that will appear of the Friday afternoon...

'I don't hand out Personal Information,' he says, '...so I just gave him a Postcode, a Street and a House Number.'

That's sounds Personal Enough, I tell him.

'That's only Personal to the House, not you, McEarly,' he says, 'I'm not without the compassion. I never told him you were Jewish.'

I'm not Jewish.

'You see McEarly, I have so little Personal Information about you how could I give the man any at all?'

You've been more than fair, I say, but if he comes back will you tell him I left?

'That'll cost you a ten pound note,' he says.

I haven't got one.

'Then give me the watch.'

Your brother has it.

'That's alright then,' he says, 'As long as it's in the family.'

'Who are you?' says Dealy. ...and I look around for the rupture in the Fabric of Space/Time.

McEarly.

...surely he remembers this willing ear...

'Mc *Feck'n Absent*,' says Dealy, 'Where the *feck* have you been. Look at these *feck'n* coffins I made on *My Feck'n Own. Who's* going to *feck'n* stack 'em?'

I will, I tell him.

...and while he puts on the kettle I'll stack all three...

'Look at you,' says Dealy, 'Three years here with every chance to make your mark and what happens when you go missing? Nothing. It's like you never been.'

I'm a simple man, I tell him, Low Impact is the Life's Motto. An Indian couldn't track my Carbon Footprint.

'And what would happen if you left?'

If I'd left why would I care?

'I'll tell you what,' says Dealy, '*Feck'n nothing.* There'd still be the requirements of coffins leaving this yard even without the mournful shadow you cast across it.'

Has there been a Cure for Cancer while I've been gone?

'And what *feck'n* time do you call this?' says Dealy, 'A week off and then you have the *feck'n* audacity to be *feck'n* late.'

I look at the wrist but the watch is now as irredeemable as the reputation I have built up over three years.

'My fingers are to the *feck'n bone,*' he says.

…and the lungs to the gluepot and the head to a suitably resin-enhanced stupor…

'Why have you come back? I was getting on well without you.'

So you're allowed back in the cabin?

'No …but it was only a matter of time.'

I didn't mean to interrupt your career trajectory.

'Too *feck'n* right, McEarly. Watch your *feck'n* step.'

The cabin door creaks ajar. The foreman shouts, 'McEarly. I want you.'

Dealy glares at me.

'Don't you *feck'n dare,*' he says.

'McEarly!'

Dealy's toes are up against mine.

I have to go, I say, A Lack of Employment beckons.

The door closes behind me with the eyes of Dealy charring the timber.

'Sit down, McEarly.' The Foreman moves the paper from the table …turning over the crossword as he does. 'Do you take the sugar in your tea?'

…and is this the shiny coating on the bitter pill…

No, thank you.

He slams tea from a mashing can into a spare lid and slops it with the sleeve of his shirt.

'It concerns your Employment,' he says.

I thought it might.

'You've had several unenforced absences over the last two weeks.'

It depends on your perspective, I say.

He picks up the paper... turns it back to the crossword and puts it down again.

'Productivity,' he says, '…has suffered greatly.'

…and there's a queue of deceased outside the Co-op stiffening in the vertical rain…

'And it can't go on,' he says.

I was thinking of handing in the Notice anyway, I say.

…I push the tea away and start to get up…

'Sit down, McEarly,' he says, 'So that's why I'm firing Dealy.'

You can't do that.

I reach again for the tea and he spikes my wrist to the table with his Devil's Fork.

'I can do what I like, McEarly.'

But what about his wife?

'What about her?'

The woman is not prepared for a twenty-four-seven burst of Dealy.

'That's their problem.'

No. I'll leave. It's the only choice.

…before the unenforced becomes the enforced …and then the running and the leaving behind to leap the falls and the ladders to find the pool of eternal rest…

'Do you know how many coffins he made while you were off?'

…of course I know…

Three?

'The same three. He keeps moving them around the yard.'

Put me in charge of him, I say.

'He's not a Crossword Puzzle.'

Oh yes he is.

'Dealy? Come in here.'

Our paths cross at the cabin threshold.

'It was only a matter of time, McEarly,' says Dealy, 'I *feck'n* told you...'

Dealy's cap is clutched in his hand. He will not look at me and his feet shuffle further into the mulch by the mill.

I'm taking you off the gluepot, I tell him.

'Yes, Mr McEarly,' he says.

And I'm giving you the saw.

'Thank you, Mr McEarly.'

And if you call me Mr McEarly again I might just *feck'n* hit you.

'That's what's been missing around here, Mr McEarly,' says Dealy, 'A bit of *feck'n Authority.*'

Dealy? These planks are too thin.

'Too thin? Too thin for what?'

You'll never make a joist with these.

'I'm not making a joist,' he says, 'I'm making us a *feck'n* cabin.'

…and I'm wondering how much a subscription to the New Scientist will cost me come payday…

Moby Chick

O'Daly beckons me and slides his blonde hair to the window so I can take the seat he's been saving. The crossword is upon us in a flick of the paper …the pencil already behind his ear and waiting…

…I scan the clues…

Start with four down, I say, 'Investiture'. Eight and two. Try 'swearing-in'.

'Trust you to know about the swearing.'

Fourteen across is 'Colombo' and twenty-seven down is 'Forfeit'.

'Slow down,' says O'Daly, 'This is a fifteen minute bus ride and I would like to try one myself.'

I lean a finger and tap. Try that one then…

…and while he's pondering, the rest fall sleeping into the matrix, nesting in little paper cradles and letters shuffling to fit…

'Here…' he says, pushing the paper onto my lap, 'Just keep the writing consistent. I can't have my reputation at the Poly destroyed.'

What did you say your Degree was?

'Sociology.'

I think you're safe, I tell him.

'Why's that?'

...over the last three years I have come to enjoy our moments of ante-meridian cruciverbalism and would not willingly allow my misplaced honesty to spoil it...

You're Unassailable, I tell him.

'Which one is that?'

Twenty-two across. Do you know anything about Tinkers?

'Interesting Social Phenomena,' he says.

Is it compulsory to have the red hair?

'As a Tight-Knit but Solitary Community they occupy a limited gene pool.'

But when they travel?

'They take the pool with them,' he says.

So the red hair stems from a pure strain?

'All the way back to Leif Erickson.'

And there's no dilution of the waters?

'You don't piss in a Tinker's Pond,' says O'Daly, 'Not twice...'

But if you were the person adapted, I say, and promised never to dilute the gene... What then?

'You'd be a queer kind of fish to want to swim alongside *them*,' says O'Daly. 'And with that black thatch of yours you'd stand out a mile. You wouldn't last two minutes.'

...but Cod like me are silver ...and such mournful eyes are beyond rejection as we sail with mouths wide open missing nothing...

'They'd have you for breakfast.' he says.

Before I get up from the seat I scan the gates of the timberyard for a flash of orange tweed.

'What's the matter, Julius?'

O'Daly is the only person I allow the use of my full and personal name. We share the same ecological niche in that we're both a fraud ...his degree is from a college in Illinois with only the barest brush of the postmark left upon it ...and I'm Julius McEarly.

I can't be too careful, I tell him, there is a Game Afoot.

'Does it have to do with Tinkers?'

Only in that whichever way I look I find either Tinkers or Tankers and I'm running out of space in which to turn.

'What time shall I put by the crossword today?'

Make it fourteen minutes and seventy-two seconds.

'Can that be right?' he says.

Show it to the Maths department. Tell them it confirms a hitherto-unproven Fibonacci Sequence. They'll spend the next eight hundred years trying to prove you wrong.

'What have they been doing the last eight hundred?'

Trying to prove you right.

'Jeezus, Julius. The Interconnectivity of Life is Astonishingly Boundless.'

It's more than that, I tell him, ...for outside the window is a flash of the tweed under a green umbrella... It's also becoming Astonishingly Personal.

...and as the bus draws away from work again with me still on it there is a flurry of currency issuing from the exhaust ...and the further we travel the more expensive it gets...

'Are you not at work today?'

I thought I'd take a Sabbatical.

'Julius,' O'Daly turns in his seat to face me and there is a worry behind his blue eyes, 'Will you let me help?'

I left you eighteen down... 'naïve' ...eleven letters third one 'I'.

'I am Uninitiated in your mysteries, McEarly.'

...and he doesn't need my help in bogging down his life. ...for he wrestles the Mysteries of Education by day ...and this is the first time in two years he has called me by my surname and I wonder does this signal a sea-change in our relationship?

You need to take the Circle Route, I say, The extra half hour on the bus will see the puzzle finished without me.

'Julius!' he says.

…and the half of the bus that was not already watching turns to stare…

…and the fins fall silent …the tail quiescent…

'Stop, Julius.'

…and in his eyes this has become a plea for clemency …for release from the constant bicker of my apprehension…

I have stopped, I say, but is a fish still a fish if it no longer swims?

'Julius,' he says, '*We* are taking a Sabbatical.'

The bus stops outside the Poly and we are resolute in our fastness.

Where are we going?

'I don't care,' he says.

Will you not be missed?

'Julius,' says O'Daly, 'I'm a Sociology Lecturer. If I'm not at work… please kindly tell me who gives a *feck*?'

Can I be honest with you?

'Of course,' he says, 'What did you want to say?'

Nothing. It was a rhetorical question.

We get off the bus into a Wild Part of Town and it's quiet. The streets are empty except for last nights chip papers and curry cartons. Bits of re-incarnated Doner Kebab adorn the copings of a low brick wall beside us as we scan the pavements for any sign of movement.

'I'd heard rumours of Life here,' says O'Daly.

The Mars Rover wouldn't be out of place, I say, and think of the saving.

'What time is it?' he says.

I study my empty wrist…

About eight thirty, why?

'I'd heard that from eight o'clock onwards this area was a Den of Iniquity.'

And is that what you're looking for?

'I don't know what I'm looking for,' he says, 'Only that I'm looking.'

How will you know when you've found it? I say.

'Did you not know,' says O'Daly, 'that Dame Fortune has teeth?'

Is that the Dame Good Fortune or the other kind? I ask.

'The both,' he says, 'One bites your heart and the other bites your arse.'

How do you tell which is which?

'The Good one bites your arse,' he says, 'That kind of wound heals.'

...and he casts around for something he seems to have misplaced ...everything falling under his wavering gaze...

What have you lost? I say.

'Inspiration,' he says, 'I'd hoped that being here would be enough on its own ...that unbounded torrents of felicity and mayhem splashing from the very doorways and windows would seep into my recoiling soul and lubricate some of the parts of me that seem to have seized through disuse.'

Such as?

'Such as the Laughter Muscle,' says O'Daly, 'So rarely subjected to the Dynamic Tension it remains a seven-stone weakling.'

Can I see it?

'No, you can't,' he says, 'You'd only kick sand in its face.'

From along the street comes the sound of a shutter being rolled up. Behind it is a glass case with a series of parallel bars. A man slides chicken carcasses onto the bars and presses a button to set them rotating. A warm glow builds behind the glass until it envelops the chickens. We walk up to watch.

'Just look at them,' says O'Daly, 'That Golden Light. It's Ethereal. It makes me think of their little souls being sucked up into Heaven as I speak.'

Are you sure it's Heaven? I say, They're breaking out in a sweat.

'Wouldn't you with a pole up your arse?' he says.

He presses his nose against the glass and sniffs.

'If it's anything to go by it *smells* Heavenly …and Praise Be to The Lord for Sage and Onion.'

The man comes out from the shop…

'What in God's name are you doing with my oven?' he says.

'You see Julius? I was right,' says O'Daly, '…and look!'

He points to the oven.

'Look, Julius…'

Inside the oven a knot has come loose in the strings trussing one of the chickens. A wing has worked free and as the carcass rotates it beckons like Ahab's arm from where he stood pinned fast and tight forever to the flank of the White Whale.

'It's an Omen,' says O'Daly, 'A Sign from Above. Help me, Julius. We must free this hapless messenger from it's predicament.'

'He was a religiously perceptive man,' says O'Daly, 'His language was so arcane as to be almost Biblical.'

And capable of great restraint, I say, The way he held on to me for the first twenty-five yards while you limped away was remarkable indeed. Now tell me what we do with an almost raw chicken?

'Well…' says O'Daly, 'Well…'

And did you not think to steal a bag too …so we could at least carry it?

'I didn't steal it,' says O'Daly, 'I Liberated it. The Allies didn't steal France at the end of the last war, did they?'

Perhaps they couldn't find a bag big enough, I tell him.

'It wouldn't have helped,' he says, 'The French already stole anything worth having.'

We are made to stand on the steps outside for half an hour until the Aquarium opens. O'Daly says hardly a word while we wait except to confirm his certainty that we were led here unerringly by the chicken cradled in his arm. I take that time to study the posters on the wall ...comparing gill structures and the downturn-upturn jaw lines of an Order similar to my own.
I should be overwhelmed by a taxonomic sense of Family, I say, but I am not.
'Try Genus,' says O'Daly.
I'm a Wild Fish, I tell him.
'Is that Specific?' he says.
I try not to be, I say, it's so limiting.

The door opens and a Person in Uniform stares out at us. He blinks in the light of a brightening day, absorbed by the dampness that has meanwhile settled upon us.
'I was expecting the School Party.'
'They've nothing to celebrate,' says O'Daly, 'Trust me...'

The air inside is heavy with moisture rising from the tropical tanks. O'Daly steers me around them ...fish follow our every step with unblinking eyes that penetrate the overcoat to the scales beneath and the smiles are fixed and the applause of gills muted from respect. He leads me down a glass tunnel and we stop to stare up at pale bellies.
'There are Grazers...' he says, pointing out flatfish burying their wise heads in the sand, '...and Sifters...' Rays drift past ...inverted clipper ships in full ribbon sail, '...and there are Hunters.'
Circling Sharks glass-eye the chicken carcass he holds aloft in the curious dry.

And which one am I?

'Not a one of them,' he says, 'Follow me.'

The overcoat is tightening for the tank now beside us draws warmth from the bones wrapped within.

'Welcome Home,' says O'Daly.

Are you sure your Degree is not in Sagacity? I say.

'They will put on it whatever you are prepared to pay for,' he says.

Then tell them to only put on it The Truth.

'Then it would be empty.'

It never could be.

…for in front of me codlings swim in synchronised ecstasy and each twist and turn repeats itself along my willing spine and I'm the unblinking stare returning a volley of unblinking stares through the glass…

'Julius…' says O'Daly, 'Your mouth is open.'

…I close it …and salt spills from the gums and the hard-edged pallet-bone and there is a reed at the corner of my lip I spit clear…

How did you know?

'While teaching Sociology from a book you learn something, Julius.'

Like what?

'Like Sociology,' he says.

'I'm sorry,' says the Assistant, 'You can't bring your own food in here.'

'This is not food.' O'Daly holds the chicken aloft, 'Do you not recognise a Repatriated Soul when you see one?'

'I don't care what Religion it is,' she says, 'If you don't take that *feck'n* chicken out of here I'll feed you to the Shark.'

O'Daly holds it out to her as a peace offering.

'And don't you *dare* put it on my *feck'n* counter,' she says.

'Can you not help me find a secure place of Asylum for it?' he says.

'What was wrong with the one you escaped from?' she says.

O'Daly turns to me …crest so obviously fallen…

'Julius,' he says, 'Who would have thought that saving a soul could be so burdensome?'

It only weighs a kilo, I tell him, put it in the bin.

'Such Ignominy,' he says, 'Fain we are in Death as in Life.'

Now wash your hands, I say, for its intelligence is seeping in through your skin.

The café is a potential clatter of empty chairs where we sit frozen for the sake of silence. Our overcoats are on the radiator and the coffee is hardly warm enough to drink.

'Julius,' says O'Daly, 'You must promise to be careful.'

This I can promise.

…it fits the comfortable coffin but there are others around who would slide their wishes and hopes and dreams in amongst us until there is nowhere left for a Cod to swim…

'Good,' he says, 'For I would hate to lose you.'

You're not Sheary, I say, A man careless with Wives and Dogs.

'No, I'm not Sheary. Though wives and dogs continue to elude me.'

Do you have the wish of either?

…and from the moment of pause I can tell that the loneliness has not managed to keep its distance…

'No…'

Then how do you see your age? There are only so many Crossword Puzzles in the World.

'I'm a Conservationist,' he says, '…and an absence of Wives and Dogs can only further the Conservation of My Immortal Soul.'

To what end?

'That's the Great Adventure, isn't it, Julius. The Great Adventure.'

I think the Path might be a little eroded by now, I tell him.

'That's why I'm in no great rush,' he says.

There is granulated salt in a tiny white pot and I think it's the sugar but somehow it seems more appropriate to the day so I drink the coffee straight down.

'You know, Julius,' says O'Daly, 'Once you numbered by the Million.'

He shakes his head …and there reflected in the glass table is the sorrow I never sought to see.

What happened to me?

'You were Hunted,' he says, '…almost to Extinction.'

Why?

'Because you were different. Because you were intelligent enough to breed and grow and speed and dart and all those other marvels that the rest of us can only be the pale reflection of.'

You see that? You look at me and you see that?

'Not only me, Julius. There are others that see you, too.'

And what do they see?

'They see a man who needs Love and Freedom as part of a balanced diet. They see a strength in there buried deep under a counterfeit of scales and they hope you find it before you drown.'

Tell me something, O'Daly, am I the one holding up you, or are you one the holding up me?

'I can do no more than tread water beside you, Julius. For I have a weight that keeps dragging me under.'

Then let me take it.

'I can't do that, Julius. It might sink you.'

What is there could be that heavy?

…and for the first time today I see the familiar smile that graces him when he beats me to an answer…

'I know who you are, McEarly.'

…and now he's the Torpedo Fish with inherent lightnings …and I'm safe only so long as I swim …so I slip my mind away with the Silkies into the Sanctity of a Hebridean Sea…

'Why did you not just stay, Julius?'

And since when did anyone ever take 'no' for an answer?

'I have something for you,' he says.

Out comes the wallet from the pocket and it's dark and shiny and pressed together against the notes I may have to borrow for the coffee.

He fins through the plastic folders and can't find what he wants. He tips the lot onto the table and the glass swims with Chiropractors Telephone Numbers.

I pick up a card and turn it in my fingers…

Dr. Benson. Osteopath.

I turn it again so it faces him.

'Lower spine,' he says, 'Old College Injury.'

You never went to the College.

'When the Degree arrived it came through the letterbox and like a fool I bent to pick it up.'

It was heavy with The Truth.

'It was heavy with the Bullshit.'

The separation of the two is only a matter of Perspective and Lumbar Vertebrae.

'Here…' he says …and holds out a folded paper with lightly crimped edges.

I start to open it carefully along the folds. He puts out a hand to make me pause.

'This is a gift, Julius. I hope it doesn't betray the giver for he would never betray you.'

I open the paper and a face stares back at me. A million tiny dots shoaled together to produce a likeness…

'Did it itch?' he says.

Everywhere, I tell him, The whole skin became untenable.

'I meant the beard,' he says.

A beard is Specific, I tell him, I'm done masquerading as a Catfish.

I fold the paper and push it back into his hand.

He pushes it back, 'Take it, Julius. For all I know it's the only one in existence.'

Keep it, I say, Keep it tight in the pocket and when Experience fails to dislodge the Bullshit, take it out and remember a friend.

'You're not leaving, Julius?'

I may have to …but before I go I have a gift for you, too.

I place it in the centre of the table.

'Thanks, Julius. I always wanted an odd sock.'

Look in it, I tell him.

His fingers roll back the top of the sock in the neat way that I can see them doing every single morning while he sits at the edge of his single bed in his single room with the single radiator and single rack where he has them draped in singularity for the matching of them matters only to the eyes of other people.

The spring steel and card clatter to the glass.

'What is it, Julius?'

It's a Get Out of Pain Free card, I say, Except it's not Free.

He picks up the card and spins it to read.

'Nurse Shaughnessy? Is she on the Health?'

No. But she comes faster than an Ambulance on 112.

'Is she the expert on Orthopaedics?'

If you have a bone of any sort she can stiffen it.

'And the cycle clips?'

I am not licensed to initiate you further in the ways of Nurse Shaughnessy. These are things best left unknown until the right occasion.

He slips the clips into the overcoat pocket behind him.

'What if it fails to arise?'

It never will, I say.

The Truth is Out There

'In case it slipped your notice, Mr McEarly…'

…if it has it will be rectified before nine forty-five because Ignorance is become Dealy's Eighth Deadly Sin…

'…we have been Invaded!'

Rain drips incessant from the canvas over us, turning the yard into a bog of shavings that mulch underfoot. Dealy and I are still barred from the cabin …Dealy because of his mouth …and me because of …well …my mouth.

Are they wearing the raincoat, I ask, for they'll be no use here if they're not.

'You won't be mocking when they creep up and slit your throat in the night, Mr McEarly,' says Dealy.

…not even if they have my House Number, Street and Postcode…

By what sign shall I know them?

'Don't get *feck'n* Biblical on me, Mr McEarly I know you're one o'them Orthodoxicals.'

Atheixicals …if you don't mind. …for the cod has gills.

'Whatever you say, Mr McEarly. But you can't tell me that you haven't noticed the Invasion.'

I had a flat once that had ants …and another with mice although I never saw one.

'They're Extra-Dimensional Beings,' says Dealy.

Ants?

'Mice.'

That explains the Holes.

'Trans-Dimensional Pathways,' says Dealy, 'They suck in all the odd socks and missing watches and things you can't find.'

Are Tinkers Trans-Dimensional? I ask.

'Of course,' he says, '…for they have no boundaries at all.'

So how do we defeat the Mice?

'With Traps.'

So Flaherty's Hardware is the Centre of Logistics from which we shall repel this Invasion?

'No… no… Mr McEarly, for that would only rid us of the Mice.'

I thought you wanted to be rid of the Mice?

'I do…' he says.

Especially the ones who have learned to hold a nocturnal razor?

'No, no, Mr McEarly,' The Lardy Cake finds itself stamped into the mulch… 'It's not the *feck'n* Mice.'

The Ants?

'It's the *Feck'n Women.*'

I don't know how to say this, Dealy, but…

'Just *feck'n* say it, Mr McEarly. We all know you're *feck'n* stupid.'

Women have been around for a while, I say, To the best of my recollection there are at least fifty percent of us of that persuasion.

'*Feck'n* typical,' says Dealy, 'You take the most sophisticated argument and crack it with a hammer. You Atheixes are all the *feck'n* same.'

Except when we're Jewish.

'You're not *feck'n* Jewish, Mr McEarly. How many times do I have to tell you?'

I'm a man that likes assurance, I tell him.

'Then make sure it's fully comprehensive,' he says.

The Lardy Cake bears a mournful lopsided grin where the bread has folded under Dealy's foot. He studies it with a wistful eye.

'You make me so *feck'n* mad, Mr McEarly.'

I don't know how much help I am, I say, but I'm happy to do my bit.

'Just listen to me…'

I can do this.

'What do you know about the Hive Mind?'

I'm never sure about my own so I'm unqualified to understand anyone else's.

'Bees are a case for study,' says Dealy, 'Every swarm has a Central Locust from which they swarm and every bit of knowledge they find out they share when they get back …and like it or not, Mr McEarly …you're the *feck'n* Locust.'

No, I tell him, I'm an Atheix Cod. I never had the time for insects.

'What Planet are you from, Mr McEarly?' he says, 'You pitch up here three years ago and I know no more about you now than I did then and you're still as *feck'n* ignorant.'

Perhaps I need a better teacher.

'I do my best,' says Dealy …he stirs bread into the mulch with the toe of his boot… '…but there's only so much power in the one Lardy Cake.'

You're being restricted by the Woman You Married, I say, starvation can be an effective way of holding back an Innate and Springing Intelligence.

'A conspiracy, you say?'

…he studies the yard for a moment …and the slick where the oil from the lardy cake drifts petroleum reds and greens into an adjacent puddle…

'No …for she doesn't have the ginger hair.'

The ginger hair?

'I thought that might make you sit up, Mr… Mc… *Feck'n*… Locust… *Feck'n*… Early. Wherever you go there's this swarm of ginger-haired women always hoovering in the background.'

…and I wonder if he would like one …or three…

Are you jealous? I ask.

'No,' he says, 'My throat is safe from the razor. My head from the frying pan is another matter but that's just a marital expression of care. I want to know why you do it. Are you the Vanguard?'

The Truth Is Out There, I tell him.

'Problem is,' says Dealy, '…so are you.'

Strike One

'You took your time getting home, McEarly,' says Shel, 'My Da' wouldn't like that.'

Perhaps we should synchronise diaries to avoid future contusion.

'You haven't the pages in yours,' she says.

I'd invite you in but it doesn't seem …seemly.

'I don't mind if you stay on your doorstep, McEarly.'

She reaches up the lintel for the spare key, 'I'll make the tea. Wait there.'

She comes back to the door where bemusement lays around me thicker than the paint on the step.

'Have you a coin for the meter?'

I shake my head.

'I'll put one back then,' she says.

The tea is hot and sweet and bitter with the certainty that nothing but my breath remains my own. I have no sole property without fingers exploring or eyes a-coveting and any sense of personal accomplishment is a far distant land that may yet be a mirage.

'What are you smiling at, McEarly,' says Shel.

I was writing my Will.

'Da's been struck,' she says.

…a JCB at the very least …for nothing flesh and bone has a hand the size that would topple Benigglety…

'He's up at the Hospital.'

Then why aren't you with him?

'They sent me to get you.'

This is not the seriousness, is it?

'The nurse said he'd only been struck mildly…' She shuffles the heels of her palms into the orbits of her eyes and they come away wet. '…so perhaps they don't like him much there.'

Is he awake?

'Yes …but his left eye is slid down like the sauce on a Mr Whippy.'

This tea is good. I could do this every day.

'No, you couldn't, McEarly,' she says, 'It wouldn't be seemly.'

The bus driver stares at the pile of meter coins on his tiny shelf but takes them and punches out two tickets.

Shel's hand steals into my own and strips away the layers that have accumulated my life until the throat of it lays bare and tiny teeth sink sharp points into the skin and pause just inside the threshold of notice …there is no tearing …no red-painted rending of flesh …yet I am dumb with sensation…

I look down and she is watching me …feathers wisp her mouth but these are pure and white without the frequency of a lie …her eyes close wet and the teeth sink.

Benigglety is up in the bed like a picture frame dropped on one corner. His left eye is rheumy and leering. The right is still the hammer it always was.

'Mang Lary,' he says.

McEarly, I say.

…I realise that correcting Benigglety is akin to climbing in a tiger's cage but the nurses have the sheets so tightly tucked I think even he can't escape…

'Az rhwat I zed,' he says, 'Gum glosa…'

What for?

'I rhant ya do feer de 'and o me,' he says.

I do.

…I can promise him that …I fear it on my arm …my head …and severally on my ribs…

Shel pushes me from behind until my trousers touch the bed beside him.

'Feel,' she says, 'He said *feel*…'

Benigglety reaches up and takes the hand that Shel is still nibbling. He covers them both with his to crush us together.

'Uu… ttil am reight,' he says.

Shel pays the bus fare and I start to tell her it's too much but the fingernails strike deep into the flesh so I shut up.

'Sit down, McEarly,' she says, 'I'm taking you home.'

Can I have the window seat? It's a favourite of mine.

…with the world going by at such a speed it helps me to understand why inertia rips my arm off every time I try to grab something I'd like…

'I'll take the aisle seat,' says Shel, 'It's quick for the exit.'

The sky leers past us in patched irregularity. Darkness is falling east of the town and street lamps spring with buds of orange that never quite flower the cascade of night.

Where are we going?

'We're there now,' says Shel.

Where's there?

There is a concentrated gravitational mass in this slender body that lurches me to my feet. Off the platform, my feet shift and churn on gravel. The door shishes and the bus swifts away reflecting the glow of a single lamp and this is nowhere …and I'm in the middle of it.

With a Fox firmly attached.

I pull up our footsteps…

Look at me, I say.

I tug her around by the hand so she faces me in the dark of the passageway and stare into her eyes …and for a second I think it's the flash of the fin …but slowly it focuses into the half-moon deep in the black of her…

What am I, Shel? And don't you think it unusual to be holding the hand of a stranger in the dark of the night land where anything might happen?

'Don't worry, McEarly,' she says, 'I won't let anything happen to you.'

That's all right then.

'You're *my* McEarly, now,' she says.

…and the knuckles of her right hand streak into my solar plexus …I double to my knees and she tugs me back upright again…

'That seals it,' she says.

Will you promise me something, I gasp.

'Anything, McEarly.'

Don't ever stop liking me …for I fear the emotional re-kindling.

The hedges either side are trimmed by moonlight into black shadow and spear green where it strikes the leaf gloss. Shel tugs my hand and I'm looking for the scuffed soil and worn-out grass of the entrance to her earth where in the short breath of five years the Hounds will pack to bay wild lunacy…

You didn't answer me.

'Do you consider yourself dignified, McEarly?'

Well…

'Then why should I dignify you with a reply?'

Are you in some arcane manner related to Dealy?

'No.'

Then where did you get this elucidatory education?

'Everyone has books, McEarly.'

Including you?

'We don't have room to keep books. We read everyone else's.'

Do you also make the tea while you're reading?

'Only at your flat.'

Then that accounts for the leanness of the caddy.

I stop and haul her around...

You read *my* books?

Shel looks up at me and the night air swallows black into her eyes while the moon steps willingly aside.

'McEarly,' she says, 'You're so predictable.'

Then predict me. Am I a chicken?

...for I'd lately thought myself a fish ...in slip with the ocean stream and the slide of the reed ...and a craft of such silver refraction with the moon only rarely striking the scales...

'No, McEarly,' she says, 'You *are* chicken.'

The caravan is a glimmer across a field littered by the remains of fire. The ashes kick up as I walk and reek the air with burned plastic and the aftertaste of hot copper. I step through a tyre and Shel picks me up again.

Sorry. I wasn't brought up feral.

'It's in the blood,' she says.

Mine's rather thin, I tell her, I can tell by the way it's running down the inside of my trouser leg from the shin.

The caravan door is unlocked.

'Can you think of anyone would steal from my da'?' says Shel.

…the obverse list would run from Shenanigan to Shibbereen but then I see a picture of him katy-cornered against the pillow and keep my gob shut…

There are no lights on inside the caravan and the air is thickened with presences current and past with no obvious temporal join.

Shel lets go my hand and I'm lessened by the lack.

'This is Loki,' she says.

Somewhere in the blood that pounds my head is a hump of dark that stirs with the watchfulness of a dragon's eyelid. It settles again. I hold onto Shel's hand for without it the night has no foundation. The carpet beneath my feet is so deep I could sway with it.

'This is Cnut. He's twelve. And don't worry… for I have taught him the correct way to spell it.'

I never dreamed there was more than one way to spell twelve.

Shel's hand slips into mine and the teeth dig deeper into the skin.

'Under the table,' she says, '…is Ragnar.'

And you are the only girl?

'The boys do the late shift,' says Shel, They'll be up when the twins, Gudrun and Sigrid, get back from the twilights.'

Did your mother ever shop at IKEA? I venture.

'Da' said she wouldn't ever. She thought it queer they named all their furniture after children.'

I'd better go before the shift change, I tell her, You'll better explain me on your own... I've always been something of an immediate distraction.

'Now you know where we are,' says Shel, 'I don't expect you to be a stranger.'

I know where you are, I tell her, But where am I?

The Fox rags my sleeve and in the dark I come to believe that chicken wire has no incorruptible depth as I am dragged down and under.

'Home,' she says.

The door of the bus shishes behind me. In the cab is the affirmed owner of a fearfully-wronged Jack Russell. He holds out his hand and so out of practice with money have I become that I immediately think to shake it.

'One pound thirty pence,' he says.

My fingers flex the vacuum of pockets in search of the real God Particles. I hold out the watch...

'It will not fit the till,' says the driver, 'Check the jacket.'

I lift the lapel and examine the familiar fluff under the felt with which they pack out the expense of the tweed.

It's mine, I say.

'That never was in dispute,' he says, 'It's rare to see a coat fits so badly it trademarks its owner. Try the pocket.'

If the ownership of the jacket is beyond question, I say, then so is the eternal emptiness of the pocket.

'McEarly...'

Alright... alright...

...and the surprise of a blue note under the left hand ...I stare back at its lack of crispness and the rumple of swirls and faces upon it...

The driver snatches it from me to compare the number with a list clipped by his ear.

'That's fine,' he says, handing it back.

I am waiting for the ticket, I say, without which it has become illegal to travel.

'I haven't the change,' he says, 'Give me the watch.'

There is a touch of the lemon-yellow on the leather so I slide tight to the window where the moon ducks the roofs and alleys as it follows me. The bus is empty except for myself and the driver and the lingering recollection of Shel …frail and alone in a pool of Terminal light.

'Got yourself the dog yet, McEarly?' shouts the driver.

No, I say, I have been subverted by the Fox.

…and it's walking backwards into the stream and I'm a flea at the end of her nose and hoping that the water will transform me by an as-yet-Dealy-unknown alchemy back into the proud fish that swims only for the Love of the Ruby…

Death is Hereditary

I step from the bus outside the timberyard gate … and for the fourth time in as many weeks comes a loud '*Huzzah*' and the wave of a folded green umbrella.

I head for the safety of a convenient doorway until the Tantivvy canters past and there is an orange tweed suit out amongst the white lines and traffic and I squeeze deeper and the door opens behind me and there is a stumbling of Post Office bags and Pensionable Ladies in Neat Hats and a quick excuse falling from the lips.

I pretend to read the adverts stuck to the window but all the while I'm gimleted of the cracks between and watching his progress along the tarmac. Each time he looks like making it a touch of the red trips him or another impedes the stride until he gives up and crosses back again shaking his head.

'Are you looking for the job?'
What? Oh …sorry, yes I am.
Two feet below me is the whitest bud of hair that ever framed a painted smile. She's looking up and I can't believe the bright hazel of the eyes.
'I'm looking for the handy man,' she says, 'If you don't mind the part-time.'
White whiskers edge the blood scarlet of the lipstick.
Are you the Fox? I say.

There is a nudge at the hip, 'The once I was,' she says.

Do you still have the brush?

'Yes,' she says, '…but for now it only sweeps the yard.'

Teeth nibble the sleeve and Shel drags me out the door.

'What're you doing, McEarly? You were breakfast on a plate back there.'

…but only the part-time breakfast…

I watched you through the window, I tell her, How do you get to be so big and so small at the same time?

'You never saw me. I opened the door for you.'

Then who? …but I already know the answer.

'It doesn't matter, McEarly,' says Shel, '…and anyway he's gone now.'

Who has?

'The man you were hiding from.'

I wasn't hiding from anyone.

'I know. You just went in to buy stamps and find a job as a part-time gigolo.'

Do gigolo's trim the high hedge? And reach the tins from the cupboard? By the size of her there must be so many out-of-date a mere three shelves up that…

'Shut up, McEarly.'

And I'm the Clam.

'That will do for now,' says Shel.

But I would prefer to be the Cod.

'Perhaps when you grow up,' says Shel.

Wait a minute, I say, I need to go back for the stamps.

'And why would you want stamps, McEarly?'

I need to send thank-you letters to a camp of Ikean Refugees.

The park is empty as it should be at ten-thirty of a school Tuesday and the analogy with my forthcoming pay packet impresses itself through the damp slats of the bench. The grass is wild and shocking me with its green ways ...holding down the prints I made from the gate while taking nothing from Shel.

'Should you not be at work?' Shel says.

Show me your fingers, I say.

Shel holds them up. I take a sniff and there's not a taint of the gas meter about them.

'I'm having one off, too,' she says.

...and I'm remembering the way Benigglety crushed her hand into mine over the white promise of the bedsheets ...and trying to determine whose hand was the uppermost...

'McEarly ...I know you went to work this morning. Why didn't you stay?'

I'd rather not commit myself to a conversation in which I might be forced to lie.

'You do it well enough without the compulsion,' says Shel.

But that's an inner lie ...like the inner tube that swells the whole tyre into the proper shape. That's permitted.

'You can't lie to me, McEarly.'

I don't know about that, I say.

'I wasn't asking,' says Shel.

There is a cardigan thrown around her shoulders today with the sleeves fretting loose as she shifts, prying one foot with the other. The rain of yesterday has taken from her hair all taints of meters and lintel-slipped keys leaving it bright as a January fox.

Her eyes are hidden from me.

Shel?

The head shakes and hair splashes lava against her pale skin and I feel the rumble through the bench of the upheavals and magmas building deep beneath the small outward frame and I wonder will she be the Krakatoa or the slow tropic atoll when she erupts.

'Can I talk to you, McEarly?'

Only in Loco Parentis, I say, ...though I have never been properly acquainted with the language so be careful what you say.

'Then there's not much point …is there?' she says.

Can you lie to me, Shel?

'Would you like me to, McEarly?'

No …I mean …is it possible?

'Only the inner tubes,' she says.

But what if it's the inner tubes I wish to hear?

'It wouldn't help,' she says, 'It's the air inside that's the problem.'

…I feel the sky above us heavy with the pumice grey and all that weight propped on these frail shoulders…

'I should tell you, McEarly,' says Shel, 'I'm the youngest.'

…and her eyes are closed and the grass itself alive with an impending sense of the knowing…

'Do you know why people call me Shelelagh?' she says.

They lost the catalogue?

'They say I'm the club that beat my Ma to death.'

She swings her feet into the park air, kicking hard at the metal straps securing the seat beneath me.

'Da' says I came out feet first and squalling with the whole entrails of her clutched in the hand.'

…and all around your hat, you shall wear the black ribbon…

'The blood was rare and they couldn't find enough of it.'

Perhaps you had a prior knowledge of the world awaiting, I say.

She looks at me in a significant way that I should recognise …but don't.

There are days, I tell her, when I wish I'd hung in there myself. There's nothing wrong with a little reluctance when faced with a world such as this.

'You're wrong, McEarly,' says Shel, 'This is a good world …if you treat it right.'

What about the way it treats you?

'I can live with it.'

And the option is?

'I could hide from it. The way you do.'

Bruises are cheaper this way ...I promise you.

'Bruises only ever harden you, McEarly,' says Shel, 'It's what they're for.'

...and I never thought to see the carapace of a turtle swimming the grass of West Park but here it is ...with eyes breaking the surface and staring out at me for the treat of fish of which I am the one...

Dealy says...

'I don't care for what Dealy says,' says Shel, 'He runs a mile when he sees one of us.'

That's because you've invaded his sense of security. He thinks you're Trans-Dimensional Beings.

'Like the Mice?'

How do you know about the Mice?

'My hands,' says Shel. She shrugs her arms into the sleeves of the cardigan to hide them, 'I need to wash my hands.'

They look alright to me.

...and the look returns to her face and this time I take it home ...where there are shadows and there are shadows and some of them are black and some of them...

Does Ice-cream do it?

'Temporarily,' she says, '...but none of the raspberry.'

How old are you, Shel?

'I think I'm thirteen.'

Then why did you say you were eleven?

'I never did.'

...and the brain drifts sideways through conversations and she is right. I am the Master of my Own Assumption and perhaps little else...

But you let me think it. What harm was there in the knowing?

'I know how old I am, McEarly.'

Then how long is it since your Ma died?

'Work it out.'

No. You tell me …and remember the inner tubes.

'Alright, McEarly. It was eleven years ago.'

Then why did you just say you were thirteen?

'I didn't.'

The socks she has spent the last few minutes lifting up the skinny legs fall to her ankles. She kicks at the grass and it ducks away.

'I said I *think* I'm thirteen.'

That's a very Cartesian statement.

She looks up at me with a twist in her eye.

It was twenty-seven down fifth letter 'e' on the morning bus, I tell her.

'Why do you hide from the knowledge, McEarly?' she says.

The way you hide from the death of your Ma?

'If I think I'm thirteen,' says Shel, '…then it means I had her for two years before she died.'

And what would you have learned by those two short years?

'That I wasn't responsible.'

You were not responsible.

'I wasn't born responsible,' she says, 'I'm old enough to know that. I was made responsible.'

We are all responsible, I say.

'For my Ma?'

Yes …and for everyone else's Ma. If we weren't all so busy rushing headlong into Death we might take time out to change it. It doesn't have to be so persistent.

'How would you change it?'

The Principle of *How* is easy. The *Why* is more difficult. If we conquer Death …how else can we exact revenge on our children?

Shel is a shrinking expanding space beside me as we walk to the ice-cream shelter by the bandstand. Her arms are an expressive flail.

'Alright, McEarly,' she says, 'I'll buy it. But start with the easy.'

First, I say, you have to find a person who hasn't died.

'The world is alive with them,' says Shel.

I mean one who will *never* die …and then you find another and breed it out of the Human Race. Simple.

'And how do you know they will never die?'

You wait.

'For how long?'

Until you die.

UniReverse

'The Universe is running backwards,' says Dealy, 'That's what accounts for the Red Shift.'

Is that the one comes on when we clock off?

'Am I supposed to dignify that remark?' he says.

It appears that not many of my remarks are dignified so you may if you wish.

'Most men are fools,' says Dealy, 'Except some are Eddicated and some are not.'

Does an Eddicated fool know he's a fool, then?

...the Lardy Cake conducts this morning's lecture with heroic posture...

'Of course he does. What do you think an Eddication is for?'

What about the rest of us?

'You're all fools,' he says.

The tea has gone cold, I tell him.

'No it hasn't,' he says, 'It's just warming up.'

Then why does it feel cold?

'It's subjective,' he says.

Will it be ready by the time the Red Shift gets here?

'Alright, Clever-clogs McEarly, prove me wrong.'

...before I came to work this morning I had the fair expectation that anyone with a skewed opinion of The Universe was obliged to prove it to *me*...

From memory, I say...

Dealy snorts, 'What memory might that be? What's in that head of yours?'

Sardines.

…and they're silver and red-shifted in the sediments of sauce with no eyes to worry the marvels of the Universe. No wonder they swim so willingly to the tin…

'What happens when you drive…' says Dealy.

I point out that the handling of vehicles is an art lost to me. Someone gave me the wrong address for the School of Driving and I never plucked up the courage to find it again.

'I seen you out on the road,' he says.

…I think the Lardy Cake is signalling a left turn but the study of such semaphoric dexterity is far behind me…

I never…

'I seen you in the car with Kayla Shaughnessy.'

I assure him that was a merely transient position.

…like the one we found in the back seat that cramped the leg and took a week for the recovery…

'What happens,' says Dealy, '…when a car comes up against a red light?'

I think to say it would stop …unless you're sixteen with a Tinker's hands on the borrowed wheel.

'Well,' he says, 'The Universe has hit the red light.'

What if it had been green?

'It would have expanded forever,' says Dealy.

Like the elastic in Shaughnessy's knickers?

'I would no longer have the knowledge,' he says, '…and I know whom I have to thank for that.'

I didn't expect to find gratitude at nine thirty of a sawmill morning…

'When a car stops at the red light,' he says, '…and all the others pile up behind it …they all have their little red lights on. Wherever you look in the Universe that's all you can see …brake lights.'

But if it was running backwards wouldn't they all have their little reversing lights on?

'Here's the switch,' says Dealy, 'Direction and time are purely subjective and all of them cars think they're going forwards but...'

So when I push a log through the mill ...what I've really done is pull two planks through the other side and stitched them together with the blade?

'Exactly.'

Then can we run a sweepstake on when the foreman gets his fingers back?

Chandelier

'McEarly,' shouts the foreman, 'There's a 'Person' at the gate for you.'

There is a flash of fox through the gap in the fence and I pour the last of the hot glue into my hand without the benefit of the glove.

'McEarly!'

I hope he has the moment while I work my way through a grimace…

Coming…

'So's the Christmas.'

He's watching the gentle scrape of my hand to leave the skin intact, 'What are you doing?'

Trying not to take work home. It's the insurance you see.

'McEarly …come with me now.'

Shel is tugging my hand but the feet are reluctant to cross the line where paid employment ends and the entrepreneurial freedom of financial disaster begins.

'It's Sheary,' she says.

What about him?

'Kayla Shaughnessy thinks he's dead.'

How can she tell?

…and I recall the various ways of pneumatic resuscitation practised by District Pseudo-Nurse Shaughnessy on the many and intricate levels of intoxication …and if she can't get him up then…

Where is he?

'He's at home.'

Why did Shaughnessy send *you*?

'She was trying to get his motor running,' says Shel.

Ok. But I need to clock off.

I put the card in the rack but it won't stay. Shel grabs my other hand and I jog off with her to the one hand and a clock card glued to the other.

Sheary is hanging from a rope tied to the banister. Three feet of clear air blows between his feet and the tiles and if I could do this without the obligation of fatality I can see it as a much easier way to get around my flat.

Kayla Shaughnessy is on the front step with head in hands and a cloak of weariness I never knew she had draped around those beautiful rounded shoulders.

'I tried to resuscitate him,' she says, '…but I was too late.'

Does that account for the trousers around his ankles?

'I tried to lighten him,' she says, 'So the rope didn't …you know …but I couldn't get them off over the cycle clips.'

He knew you were coming, then?

'I was an hour late.'

Not like you? I venture.

'Nursing is not an exact science,' she says.

I thought it was …since the Kinsey Report.

'Customers are like buses,' she says, '…with some of them you get nothing for ages and then they come all at once.'

And Shel?

'She was here when I arrived.'

Amongst other things I'm aghast. At the end of Shel's nose appears a tiny black button and the wisps of a lie between her teeth like pin feathers. She sits down beside Kayla and I'm amazed at how far feral arms will wrap themselves around this tiny body.

'I was working the meters,' says Shel.

And what else, I ask.

'Just the meters,' she says, 'If you like I'll go home and fetch my diary.'

Sheary is rotating slowly as the rope stretches. In half a turn his foot catches the stair rail and sends him back to keep pace with the conversation. For a man with no sport in his blood he'd be good now for the watching of tennis and his eyes are wider than I ever saw upon his face and the lips shaped into memory with a snarl of '...*why don't you...*'

Are you sure that's the whole of it?

'Look at me, McEarly,' Shel stands up ...arms wide, 'How old do you think I am?'

...and I don't know...

Eleven? Forty two? Ninety?

She scowls at me from the step.

It depends on the light, I tell her. Now sit down. How come you both turned up?

A glum silence halts the slip and slither of conscience and the inevitable mix of blame-shifting words for which the Garda have the sifting reputation.

'We run a shift system,' says Shel.

Is it red?

'I stay home that week,' says Shaughnessy, 'I work over the rest to compensate.'

'And when she leaves them whooshing out the zeds I come by an hour later and work the meters,' says Shel.

She shakes her head and the brush slips the rubber band at her neck and a misplaced sense of her vulnerability doubles.

So you arrived together?

'I'm noted for it,' says Shaughnessy.

The Garda are there in a flash two hours after I ring on Sheary's phone …there being no hurry if your man is already well gone …but the clock is ticking at work and the card is still attached to my hand and if I soak it loose all the hours I have stamped on there will swim like feisty codlings into the entropic drain of my financial life.

Attached to my sleeve is a Feral Fox and although it has only the fingers in the cloth it feels more like teeth when I try to shake it loose.

This isn't right you know, Shel.

'Da' says it's alright to hold on to a man if it stops him hitting you.'

I'm not going to hit you, I say, I never would.

'That's because you don't like me enough yet,' she says.

…and her feet give a little skip the way foxes are said to dance in the beams of the moon when she is full of the skirts and the night is rare with silver…

'Take me to the park.'

I have the work to get back to, I tell her.

I hold up the card in my hand as witness. Shel rips it off and pushes it through the railings.

'Now you'll have to go and get it,' she says.

I might choose to throw you over.

'I'm an Irish boomerang,' she says, 'I might choose to not come back.'

The bench is damp from the mist and while my backside is soaking Shel is a scurry between empty slides and carousels opening for the end of the school time. She should be soaked herself but she has this way of shaking that begins at her nose and works its way down to her tail end. She shuffles backwards onto a plank swing and sits there like a moored boat rotating softly with the tide.

Do you want a push?

'I'll be alright in a minute,' she says, 'I just want to remember Sheary in my own way.'

The Sea Bed

Hello, Ruby.

'McEarly! To what do I owe this unaccustomed pleasure?'

Dealy kicked over the gluepot in a fit of existential hubris and there was no time left in the day for the warming of another.

'Is that what you do all day,' says the Ruby, '…fight?'

No, I tell her, it's not like that. As a devout coward I listen while Dealy beats my ear to the death.

The double doors of the old Workhouse pour handsome women onto the street behind us and until I met the Ruby I'd never thought of this as a good catchment area. The house prices must be doubled here. There is a blue jacket around her shoulders that I don't recognise but it's pretty enough over the limp green of a brushed calico skirt with all the day's trimmings still attached. She strokes the tiny lengths of cotton into the gutter where the wind takes them with hardly a breath of care.

'I've done three hundred and ninety two pockets today,' says the Ruby.

…I think Shel's sisters might have the edge on her there…

And was there anything in them?

'There is a word,' says the Ruby, '…that describes your capacity for humour, but for the life of me I can't recall it just now.'

Bereft.

'When I was younger…' says the Ruby.

I look at you and this is not possible…

'Shut up, McEarly,' she says, 'When I was younger I used to sometimes put a note in the pocket.'

It's an awful clumsy way to find a man, I tell her, You never know what might climb up your drainpipe dead of the night.

'It said, 'If you find this note then the trousers will always bring you luck'.'

Sheary didn't get one then.

The Ruby is quiet as we walk …the way she is while listening to the reverberations of the Mammy in the bar of a Friday. The street echoes away our footsteps until it surprises us with a new neighbourhood and clean paving and small front gardens brimming with the privacy of privet behind which the curtains don't twitch.

'I always wanted to live here,' says the Ruby.

Sell the Mammy's house.

'I couldn't do that,' she says, '…not while she's still alive.'

There are arrangements…

'McEarly…'

She punches me where the love will bloom purple and yellow on my shoulder by morning and I resolve to ask Dealy about the visual spectrum of the emotional rainbow.

'The Council.' she says, 'I rang them yesterday.'

Do they now have a place for Mammies?

…when my own was sick they offered home care for which I was to pay and out of financial consideration she allowed the cancer to slip herself away so quickly…

'They say we can have Sheary's house.'

Sheary's House?

…and the rope burns still warm to the banister and the memory of Sheary so strong I should wish good morning to him each time I went to the stair and the lips forever twisted into *…why don't you…*

'What's wrong with that?' says the Ruby.

…and the hands they couldn't unfurl in the coffin from the clutching at the rope and into each of which I could stick a candle and save on the electricity…

'The Council have cleared it,' says the Ruby, '…and redecorated the whole of it.'

…and the eyes so big as the pond frog and the following of my every movement and the window I would leave open to rid the house of the ghostly scent of Jack Russell…

'I put our name down,' says the Ruby.

There is no-one at the dog bin by the time the Ruby leads me home.

'I'd ask you in McEarly, but…'

The bus won't be long.

'Why don't you walk, McEarly,' says the Ruby, 'It'll do you good. You could lose a few pounds…'

Dealy's done that already today …for all the good it will do me.

'You're obsessed with money, McEarly,' she says, 'I never thought it of you.'

There's no point obsessing about something you do have, I tell her.

'That's coveting, McEarly. Not obsessing.'

…and I covet the lining of her jacket where it brushes the pink flimsy and the short hairs she will develop around her nipples when she's older and I can nip at with the teeth and make her laugh deep in the mirabulous throat…

…I look up to the sky to hide my expression and there are no early stars to rush above us …no trawl of the sludge-grey tapestry daylight and the moon yet hidden even from the Fox…

…my hands are itching with the contained power of the look I know I am wearing broad and plain and her eyes fix me to the damp-smelling earth so far from the ocean that I gasp for each swimming breath…

'When we have a place of our own, McEarly,' says the Ruby.

…and Sheary swings before me with metronomic regularity …and I wonder can I hold the rhythm of his death long enough to complete my leap beyond him to the spawning pool…

'You'll never believe what was stuck in the tyre,' says the driver.

I know every letter and postcode.

'You think you're *feck'n* clever, McEarly.' he says, 'But I know who you sit next to of a morning.'

Sardines, I say.

'Sardines?'

…and I smile …for only I know that in a Sidereal Dealy Dimension this has become the most Heinous of Swearings a man can utter…

Sardines it is.

I'm inside Sheary's house and the chill is bone-deep as I cross the stairway. The council would not yet give a key but Shel has told me where to find it.

'I don't like the colour,' says the Ruby, 'I've seen this lemon-yellow before somewhere…'

It's only paint, I say, but what would you do with the shadow?

'The shadow, McEarly?'

…and I think she can't see it …the trouser-less legs and the braces that sweep the floor each and every time the door opens and I shudder…

'What's the matter, McEarly,' says the Ruby, 'You look like you seen a ghost.'

I think I heard an echo.

'That's no surprise without the furniture. A few curtains and cushions will take of that.'

...and I know it was an echo of the future ...and all the curtains won't cushion that when it comes...

'I never seen you look so scared,' says the Ruby, 'Are you sure you want to do this.'

Yes, I'm sure.

...but not here and not now when movement might become the issue ...and I'm preparing the swift strokes that will allow me not to drown...

'Then is it me?'

...Oh yes, My Ruby ...it's you ...it's you as intrinsic and deep as it gets ...it's you that makes me the Foolish Cod rushing to your net of simplicity and trust ...it's you that I'm swimming so hard not to betray...

Why should it be you? I say.

...and my hand reaches out to touch the sleeve of the railway reefer and like the Good Indian I hear through the lines and sleepers to the locomotive and though it's miles away it will arrive one day volcanic with chimneys and shrivelling with blasts...

'Sometimes, McEarly,' she says, '...when you get what you want you find it's not what you wanted ...or it's not what you thought it was in the first place.'

And what did I think you were?

The Ruby looks at me directly, 'I'm not sure ...unattainable, perhaps.'

...like a Fox in a tree...

There is a smile touching my lips and it's put there by the bravado with which she graces my soul.

'You're laughing at me, McEarly,' she says.

I wouldn't do that.

'Then why are you smiling with your mouth while your eyes are clanged shut?'

Because I don't deserve it...

'Deserve what?'

...the Ruby is alive and trembling. I fold my arms around her because I'm a man in need of a hug. Her hands reach around me as if I am new and they are tempted by a thing that scares them in a way they don't understand...

...I relax into the shape of her body ...and the shades of coffins and the brightness of ginger and the loudness of *huzzahs* slip from my shoulders into the shadow of Sheary that will forever stain the tiles...

'Do you not love me, McEarly?'

...for the cod is asleep ...delved under a blanket of futures that shape and change every which way a man might turn...

Nuclear Umbrella

At the far end of the park bench Shel is a de-frocked leprechaun in leggings, ice cream and a faded tee shirt.

You understand why you're sat here with me, don't you?

'I'm not earning while I'm here, McEarly,' she says, 'So make it quick.'

Can I not take the moment to marvel at your sense of purpose, thrust as I am into the breach of civilisation as a deemed good influence?

…and where is the Ruby when I need her…

And where is my watch?

Shel holds it out and looks away and from behind I can tell she's smiling.

Thank you.

'Are you not going to thump me?' she says.

Should I?

'How else would I know that you care?'

I don't thump people I care about. Usually it's the other way around.

…I scan the park and the gates within visible reach. No sign of the Hunt…

'What you looking for, McEarly? The wife?'

…no …the US Cavalry…

I don't *have* the wife, I say.

'I seen the two of you. I was with Da' in the truck.'

I don't have the wife, I repeat.

...and hope the echo reaches back into my own dimension from which I have been severally disrupted...

'Sure and you do,' says Shel, 'Da' says you just don't know it yet.'

...and now there's an umbrella at the gates of the park and it's brown and broke like the chocolate orange and it's heading over this way ...and underneath it is the gathering of a Railway reefer jacket about to descend upon us with its breath of old sleepers and steel and I look but there's not a trace of the lemon yellow...

'Ruby said I'd find you here,' says the Beryl.

The coat, I say, It seems to have developed an instinct.

'And for God's sake, McEarly, why would *my* coat develop an instinct for *you*.'

...oh, it has ...I've seen it drag you across the other side of the street when it thought I might speak...

It might run in the family, I say.

'You mean my sister?'

She laughs horribly and the stamp of the Mammy is all across her and only waiting for the widening of the arse and I glance at Shel who sits there with no discernible expression yet her eyes are become feral.

There is a movement I don't follow ...a brush going swiftly to earth ...and I'm flummoxed as the hound.

Where is the Ruby, I ask ...and hold up my empty wrist.

'Sorry, it's a habit.' says Shel.

'It's the Mammy,' says Beryl, 'Ruby has taken her to the hospital so she won't be seeing you the night.'

...and Dealy and his Dimensions and backwards-running clocks come to steal away my moments with the Ruby ...and what about the goodwill I'm supposed to sow in this rocky little untilled outcrop at the other end of the bench ...but if Dealy is right then this has already happened and in his own words it's a case of 'pre-destinalisation'…

Don't worry, I say, I have it on good authority she'll be back before you know it.

'Oh, I see, McEarly. You have connections at the hospital now?'

The Universe is nothing if not an infinity of connections.

'I heard of your gynaecological expertise, McEarly,' says the Beryl, 'Behave yourself with my sister.'

…and I wonder what she thinks she knows of the slide and slip of silent lubricated scales between the bark of the tree and the grass of the park and the dust of the flat and the scorn of the Mammy where the poor old cod has found never a warm place for to hide through the ocean winter…

They were just a few old friends I needed to look up, I say.

'If there wasn't a child here I'd tell you to *feck off*,' says the Beryl.

'Don't mind him,' says Shel, 'He's old enough to hear that kind of language.'

'And who might you be, Madam?' says the Beryl.

'I know who you are,' says Shel, remarkable in the composure, '…and that's enough for me.'

The Beryl bristles with umbrella-laden threats of nuclear option, 'I'll give you a clip around the ear in a minute…'

'No, you won't,' says Shel, 'You don't have the initiative …or you wouldn't still live at 43 Parsley Mow Boulevard on the edge of the coal drift where the empty skips rattle slack over your garden from the trundle wires.'

'McEarly,' says the Beryl, 'Are you just going to sit there?'

…there's room on the bench between us but from the look in Shel's eye I wouldn't recommend it…

Well…

'Typical!' says the Beryl.

…and I say…

Why do you have the umbrella of a very grey but otherwise fine day?

'Just because it isn't raining,' says the Beryl, '...doesn't mean that it won't.'

Shel stands beside me in a way that doesn't even bend the grass. Watch as I might there's not ever the springing of it.

'Here, McEarly,' she says, 'Put that in your pocket.'

In the hand is a brown leather purse that swells between my fingers like a called pigeon. The Beryl is beyond the capacity of my vocals to beckon back.

'Post it to her,' says Shel.

Do you realise what this might cost me? I say.

'About a pound if you wrap it in plain brown paper. If you were a Tinker you'd make sure you took the pound from the purse first. It's called a self-funding asset.'

No, I say, What about the Ruby?

Shel shrugs, 'One day, McEarly, you will come to realise what an asset you have in *me*.'

Her ears are tufted points and the whiskers of her face and the brush lively and elastic-loose from the faded brown leggings …and just as suddenly gone…

My only hope, I say, is that you're self-funding.

Outfoxed

'Get up, Julius.'

O'Daly folds the crossword page into his bag. The bus is at a standstill in a universe of brake lights. He pushes me into the aisle and I stumble to the front by the door.

'Drunk at this time of day…' says the driver, 'There's yet two stops to the work.'

I ignore him because O'Daly has pressed the Emergency button and the door shishes open to let in the world and its volume. He takes my arm and we sweep out into a violence of exhausts and car windows engulfed in the steam of pent-up office workers.

What are we doing?

'I want to show you something,' he says.

I allow him to guide me through the tangle of emissions until we reach the footpath where he stands for a moment to catch his breath.

Are you alright?

'It's the fumes,' he says, 'I'm alright now. Come on.'

His hand tugs me in the direction of work. Placards sail past us in a frantic breath of Religious Fervour as we weave our way between.

Hold on!

…my heels dig in to stem our flow towards the timberyard…

'What's the matter, Julius? Scared?'

Damn right I am.

'Of what?'

The Tantivvy. Once you hear the Sound of the Horn you're lost.

'Run with the Fox, Hunt with the Hounds, Julius. It keeps you alive.'

Can I not Swim with the Tide?

'Only in your head, Julius. Only in your head.'

And what of the Heart?

'It's not the Heart that is the Fish.'

You're saying there's no Oil in the Liver?

'I'm saying for an intelligent man there's not much in the Lamp.'

He drags me into a doorway. The frame is green and aluminium with a step that I trip on. Beyond it are stairs leading up. He pushes me in front of him.

'Fourth floor, Julius. Wait for me there. I'm right behind you.'

He closes the door and locks it. I'm two flights up and I hear his footsteps hesitant on the treads. I go up the next two and there's a landing with windows. I wait. The hands go in and out of the pockets searching for interest in the vacuum until O'Daly pitches up beside me.

'Sorry, Julius. It's the steps.'

How old are you?

…there is a definition of grey around the eyes and a blue to the lips but the skin around them is that of a younger man…

'Forty-two,' he says.

…I listen to his breathing…

Is that in Dog Years?

'Look…'

He pushes me against the window.

Careful, I say, I have the aversion to sudden and violent movement.

'I'm asking you to look, not jump,' he says.

Beyond the window the whole timberyard opens up. The vertical railings race their sharp arrows around the perimeter like Indians at a wagon train. Dealy himself is by the gluepot …bending over to inhale in the way he always denies. The crane lowers its bill and rude pine trunks jerk to earth beside the saw and behind it are the same three coffins that I left there the week before…

'What do you see?'

Nothing.

'Exactly.'

And what was I supposed to see?

'Your Future.'

Isn't that about Choice?

'Some of us have none, Julius.'

That's Crap, I tell him.

'That's all some of us have out here,' he says.

You could have had anything written on that Degree.

'But could I have coped with it? I don't know…'

Then are you the Fox or the Hound?

'I'm the Cat stuck in the Tree of Original Thought, Julius. …and waiting for the Fire Brigade.'

I turn back to the window in time to see the door of the cabin close in Dealy's face and for once I'm sorry for him. The Student lodger his wife took in is long gone and the subscription he left behind for the New Scientist magazine has recently expired and Dealy can't justify the renewal and while I'm feeling sorry I think to transfer some of that to O'Daly…

'Don't you dare feel sorry for me,' he says, 'The look on your face is pure Jesuit.'

And you would prefer?

'Pure Bullshuit. Look out the window.'

From here we can see almost the whole way around the yard and there are foxes at strategic points of the fence. By the gate there is a tiny one and the brush is in full sway because the bus has been and gone and of course I'm treed with O'Daly here in the College's old office.

'You're a lucky man, McEarly,' he says.

I stare through the window at the absence of Hounds and the silenced clop of Horses.

Until the next Tantivvy, I say.

'The Hunt has moved on,' says O'Daly, 'Outfoxed.'

Fermanagh's Last Theorem

'It's *all* about coffins,' says Dealy.

Then your man was Irish?

'No,' says Dealy, '…he was French by Birth and Irish by Wit.'

Then he has the laugh on you, I tell him.

'Who's on the outside of the coffin?' he says.

Both of you, I tell him, If it's one of yours from the Monday morning.

'Pisstaker…' says Dealy.

…and now the Universe begins unfolding as it should…

'If a coffin equals X,' he says, '…and the lid equals Y…then…'

Whatever is in it must be Z?

'No,' says Dealy, 'Z's for nothing. That's why the Greeks called it Zero.'

'Wasn't that the Indians?'

'Listen, Mr McEarly, if you're ever to get back into the snap cabin you're going to have to curb this natural enthusiasm for impromptu conjecture.'

Five across on the morning bus …fourth letter J.

'Besides,' says Dealy, '…by the time the cowboys had finished with them that's all there was left.'

So Coffin(X) plus Lid(Y) equals Content(Z) equals Zero?

'No,' says Dealy, 'The answer is sixteen. Only an idiot can't see that. Why it took centuries to solve I do not know.'

He was French, I say.

'That would do it,' says Dealy, 'But his equation was missing the three letters.'

I'd thought he had no more than $X^2 + Y^2 = Z^2$ to work with?

'That's a very triangular argument,' he says.

Don't you mean circular?'

'No,' says Dealy, '...that was Pythagoras. The missing letters ...for which he had no space in the margin and comes as no surprise for I have seen the handbook ...are V, A and T.'

And does he give a value for those?

'Around twenty percent last time I looked,' says Dealy, 'but only if you sit down and eat your chips in the shop. Take them home and the value is Zero.'

Then it's just as well the Indians invented it.

'No,' says Dealy, 'You're missing the gist of it entire ...for they don't sell chips at the Indian ...only the curry.'

So if the cost of a coffin is equal to sixteen portions of the Friday Fish, then I think you should find a cheaper shop, I tell him.

'It has nothing to do with the fish,' he says, 'How the *feck* did fish ever come into the Last Theorem?'

Fish can be very surreal.

'That's why I never have the haddock,' says Dealy 'No. It's the pig.'

He opens the lardy cake to show me the slick lining of it.

'Stapled to the diet.' he says.

I never heard of the pig fish.

'You're *feck'n* stupid, Mr McEarly.'

...now there's an argument I've often been the product of...

'It's *all* about the pig,' he says, 'Why do you think we make coffins the size they are?'

Because God made people to fit those very dimensions?

'No,' says Dealy, 'It's for the suckling pig.'

Do they still suckle when they're six feet by two?

'Course not,' he says, 'They stop while they're still small enough to fit four to a coffin.'

Is that some kind of an instinct?

'Shut the *feck* up, Mr McEarly,' says Dealy, 'You're obstructing the Dynamic Flow of Equation.'

…Lardy Cake Numbers appear in the air between us…

'Where Coffin(X) to the power of four equals Sixteen …then…'

…Greasy Crumbs and Exponential Errors of Assumption slip free from the movement of his hands…

'Lids(Y) to the power of four also equals Sixteen.'

…and around the yard they'll stack in banked equations waiting for the Sum of a Function at which there will invariably be ham sandwiches and slices of quiche…

So where do the pigs come in?

'Ahh,' says Dealy, 'The pigs come in the coffins. Four at a time.'

I make that sixty four.

'You would …*feck'n* Mr Clever Clogs McEarly …but you don't know the half of it.'

Thirty two.

'No. The answer is sixteen,' says Dealy, '…for that's all the pigs you can get in four coffins.'

But you said there were sixteen coffins?

'Right,' says Dealy, 'But because four coffins is all you can get in an Astra van, four trips is what it takes.'

Then why not put them in a Transit all at once?

'That would be foolish, Mr McEarly, for all the Transit vans get stopped at the border …and whoever heard of smuggling pigs in an Astra?'

Is it economically viable?

'Forty five miles to the gallon if it's a diesel.'

Moth to The Flame

Moths hurl themselves at the bulb over the dog bin. They fall at my feet where I watch their stunned silence in the stunned silence emanating from the Ruby's door.

A bus halts at my loitering proximity to the stop and the door shishes open.

'A dog would soak up the loneliness, McEarly.'

The door shishes shut and the black soot rattle diminishes against the hang-nail sliver of moon where she perches the topmost rung of the night-ladder. The gutters are dry and I fear a dislodgement of scales if the Ruby doesn't soon appear from the door that watches me blind with reflection from the lack of an inner light.

Behind me there is a flash of fox and though I never catch it I hear the whoop doppler the park in my dark nightmare where grass unbends and the Beryl runs wet under a dry umbrella in pursuit of a purse that cost me the one pound sixty to post in the anonymity of brown papers and clear sellotape.

The moon spurns a wisp of insubstantial cloud and in my dream-head Sheary's Jack Russell is still running from the wheel of a Friday sardine.

Frost appears on the glass of the Ruby's door and I pull the coat tighter around myself until I realise it's just the light going on. A frosted hand lifts down a frosted coat from the frosted hook and despite the knowing there is a growing lack of heat in the bones of anticipation.

The light goes out and the door opens.

'McEarly!' says the Ruby, 'What on earth?'

I have a new job with the Council, I say, A voluntary check on the dog bins with a special remit for yours.

'I can't see you the night, McEarly,' she says.

It's too late for that.

…unless I discover that Dealy has bent light around the deep gravity well of my situation…

'It's the Mammy.'

…and through the night's oblivion comes the fast-fading scent of tree bark and the lost stain of bent grass and the two-square-yard of bed I cleared before I came out…

Turn around, I say.

The Ruby looks over her shoulder, 'Why?'

I want to see if your brake lights are on.

'McEarly,' she says, 'You can sit the bus-ride with me.'

And can I pay?

'It's expected of a gentleman,' says the Ruby.

One of us got lucky, then.

…and I think of the brown leather I so recently parcelled up stuffed with notes less the tithe for the Fox and the one pound I'd extracted for the post and the other sixty pence that left my own pocket because I'd already done the wrappings tight…

'Did you not get my message?' she says.

I think so.

…unless I misread the implied nuance of foxhound bristlings and feet stamping firmly into the soil of the park…

'Did she not say about the Mammy?'

She did …but she seemed a little distracted.

'We're all worried,' says the Ruby

…and I remember the last look from the Mammy and find myself outside of that rapidly tightening circle…

'It's the hysterectomy,' she says.
…and that's nothing to laugh about…

I don't know this bus driver.
'Where are you to the night, McEarly,' he says.
The Hospital.
'They said you were looking peaky,' he says.
…and I want to drag him from the cab and slap him with all fins until he tells me who is tugging my lead …but the Ruby pulls me away to sit near the back…
'What's the matter with you the night, McEarly?' she says.
It's the new diet, I say, Mixed metaphors are never easy to digest.

An Option To Purchase

Kayla Shaughnessy slips the bar door as if rubbed with some of her special oil.

'McEarly,' she says, looking over to where I'm nursing a halved pint. The Landlord is giving her a 'No… No…' look and the comb-over is set adrift above the surreptitious shake of head.

'It seems I have a spare slot,' she says, '…and it is the Monday.'

I bury my face in the remains of the pint to consider the options presented by Kayla Shaughnessy with a spare slot …and contortions of the cramp it might achieve.

You could double your client base, I say.

'I thought you liked my client base, McEarly?' she says.

I wouldn't have it any other way.

'Can you think right now of the *best* way?'

Have you ever tried renting eggs to chickens? I say.

'Is that a variation on a Theme, McEarly? I'm that kind of a woman for the learning.'

…and the surprise is I've always known it …Teacher …Priest …Mammy …they all said don't go near *that* kind of woman for she will have you by the nose …but they forgot to mention the wallet…

'Are you in there, McEarly?' Kayla gives my shoulder a nudge with the hot, profound cushion of her belly.

No, I say.

…I shut my eyes but behind them the Cod is slipping a reef of Shaughnessy thighs and thrusting for the taste of krill and the door opens again and it's the Ruby…

She walks over to stand by the bar, eyes drawn like the highwayman's pistols.

'Are you not coming over to buy me a drink, McEarly?' she says.

Give me a minute, I tell her.

'I don't have one, McEarly.'

The door slams behind her and I turn to look at Kayla with what I hope is reproach… but knowing full well I have the look of Sheary's dog.

Are you *that* kind of a woman, I say.

'I'm *all* kinds of woman, McEarly,' she says, 'Every single one of her. All a man has to do is call.'

Is there a number that you are all happy to answer?

'There is, McEarly,' she says, 'It's the reason you couldn't stand up.'

The door bangs behind me and a cold wind pares away to reality the early evening oncoming yellows and departing greys where flashing traffic is a two-dimensional danger to eyes peering through the distortion of a beer glass.

There's no sign of the Ruby.

I turn left by a Pizza Go-Go overflowing with empty boxes in draughty corners and there's a touch of the reefer flickering a doorway and inside it is the Ruby and inside the Ruby is the sadness for the tears are upon her face and it's too early for the moon to steal them.

I put out my tongue and her tears flood seawater back into the damaged armour of my scales …I kiss her hard …she kisses back in a way that gets hungrier with each revolution of the lips and I'm silver against the coral and pearl of her wide-open throat and the ocean is an infinity of wishes and salt-slither fins…

The reefer opens and the Ruby pulls me tight inside of it.

'You *do* still love me, McEarly. So why were you with Kayla Shaughnessy?'

I wasn't …she was with me.

'Semantics…' says the Ruby.

Perspective, I say, There's a world of difference between.

'It's not the difference between you that worries me, McEarly. It's the world of history.'

I'm tired of the rental, I say, It's never the mutual agreement you might suppose.

The Ruby looks deep into my eyes the way that makes stone weep.

'What do you want from me, McEarly? An option to purchase? Can you not just be glad of me?'

She presses me against the door barricade so hard that I rattle like a skeleton in a bucket.

'I'm not as visible as you, McEarly' she says, '…but I'm glad all the same.'

Not here, I tell her, I'm not a man for printing with the burglar-proof mesh when it's time for the fish to migrate to a warmer clime.

The key spins in her fingers with a guilty click.

'We have an hour, McEarly,' says the Ruby, '…then Beryl will be back from the hospital.'

How come you have the key?

'In case she wakes up dead one morning, someone needs to let the Co-op in.'

She keeps the casket lined and ready?

'In the bedroom, McEarly, with good Belfast soil in the bottom of it.'

How very partisan…

'In here.'

The Ruby drags me from the corridor into a small room with open curtains and the breath of her hits me with its sweetness. Hands slide across me and as they move scales drop until the whole floor is become a shimmer with silver.

'Oh …McEarly.' she says.

…and her mouth fills with the skin of my chest and the tiny springs that wind the clock of time and her teeth with my shoulder and my nose is lost in the scented chocolate of hair that smells again of the very potion I risked my freedom to discover…

She moves the length of me and the reefer is harsh against the scales and I open the collar so I can look down and watch the delicacy of her movements and explore the ecstasy of ears and elfin hollows as my fingers are lost to her head and I swim with the school of thought-fish …and the swift, wild, wish-fish inside of all women.

She looks up at me. 'Oh …McEarly,' she says.

Speak softly, I reply, I'm on the telephone.

Outside the window is a yellow-cast sky through which wires trace parallel lines. An empty skip sways the wind in wait of the morning shift and from its corner the air whips the coal-black blinding of dust onto gardens below.

In the yellow the Ruby is asleep and on the floor is a pile of scales turned cloth and creases into which I step unwillingly. Beside the Ruby the reefer nestles lonely black in the shadow of the bed for beneath it had been very little else at all.

In the hallway a hand rattles the lock the Ruby has left the key in. She stirs on the bed and I stand for a moment to watch her skin smooth with the insides of her and wait until I understand the little ridges and runnels that are the secrets and corners of her garden.

I pick up the reefer and drape it gently across her shameless feet.

The Beryl is at the door and the convulsions of her face still hidden behind the shock of seeing me.

'McEarly!'

…and she turns, for behind her is the Mammy…

The Mammy has a small suitcase by the step and I reach out to bring it in.

I stand back to usher them through the door.

'I am speechless.' says the Beryl.

'*Feck* me,' says the Mammy.

I hold up my finger.

Shush. The Ruby is asleep.

'Not murthered in my bed?' says the Beryl.

No, I say, Not *murthered*.

…and the Mammy looks at me in a queer way I never saw before…

Would you like the cup of tea, I ask.

'*In My Own House…*'

I put a finger to my lips.

'I make the tea in my own house,' says Beryl.

…and the Mammy hummphhs in a very sagacious manner…

Then I'll be having coffee.

'So will I,' says the Mammy, 'The throat is parched for words. Them *feck'n* hospitals.'

I sympathise, I say, I really do …for the look of the outside is enough to fear the internal arcanery.

'Have you ever been in, McEarly,' says the Mammy.

I only ever visit, I tell her, I'm the inveterate visitor.

'You never visited me.'

You were never in long enough to climb the list, I tell her.

'You were quick enough to that *feck'n* Tinker.'

I was called in. My name is on a roster of emergency visiting requirements.

'I'm glad the Ruby is asleep,' says the Mammy, 'For I shall speak no more of it.'

…and one of her eyes briefly closes while the other stays open…and I'm agag at the coffee…

'Watch out for the Fox,' she says.

The Beryl drags me to the kitchen, 'What did you think you were doing McEarly?'

…I wasn't thinking …I was on the telephone …and going the long distance…

'I had that room all prepared for the Mammy fresh out of hospital and now I'll have to make it over.'

…and the bed is a rumple and in the midst of it all is the smoothest, sleekest, warmest place ever found in which to hide a cod…

Can you not let her sleep a while?

'Are you mad, McEarly?'

It varies.

'Do you know the kind of trouble she'll be in with the Mammy?'

…I remember the look in the Mammy's eye. …and the closing of just the one…

I think I do.

'You don't know the half of it,' says the Beryl.

…and the chink of hall light stripes the Ruby with softness and I think that perhaps I know the whole of it …and as quick as that the knowledge is gone …and I understand that I must trawl a succession of discoveries and layer them fast to the memory so that I never forget again…

The Ruby has the warmth of the reefer outside and the comfort of the coffee inside and the expression of her face is fetching tears to my eye.

'I'm sorry, Beryl,' she says.

The Mammy is tucked up and hidden from the watching, swinging skips by the curtains I am closing. She grabs my coat and pulls me to the bed.

'McEarly,' she whispers, 'It's thirty years since I was in a bed this warm.'

And now the night around us is stepping-pools that we hop and wrap our clothes tight against the Time Encroaching.

Dealinger's Cat.

'I had a cat once…' says Dealy, '…that died of ignorance.'

That happens when you ignore things, I tell him.

'Although it's probably more true to say it died of fear,' he says, '…or maybe the both.'

Staple Diet of the Human Condition, I say.

'Don't be *feck'n* stupid,' he says, 'It was a cat.'

Fear and Ignorance only feed Suspicion, I say, Not cats.

'Listen,' says Dealy, 'while I try to Eddicate you. There's this *feck'n* great space in your head, Mr McEarly, that swigs learning beyond my capacity to deliver.'

The Lardy Cake is a white grin surrounded by oven-bottom lips and is even now looming at me through the swill of unkempt knowledge swirling into my black hole.

'This cat,' he says, '…worked its way into the mattress beneath us one night.'

What did it do with all the money it found?

'He did nothing,' says Dealy, '…for the money is in the other mattress in the spare room.'

…I make a mental note for Shel …then tear it up…

'By morning it was still there.'

The money?

'No, you *feck'n* loon. The cat.'

And where is it now?

'I don't know,' says Dealy.

Ahh.

'Ahh *feck'n* what?' he says.

It's the glue, I say, Ahh Ahh.

'Pisstaker.'

The canopy looms over us from the step where I am still banished from the cabin. In back of me is a space so black a cat could hide. I push lardy crumbs towards it and watch for a gleam in the shutter of night-eyes.

'You're not *feck'n* listening,' says Dealy.

…as that began three years ago with the commencement of my employment it's old news and I choose not to respond…

So you tried the tin of cat food by the bed?

'Have you tried to sleep beside an open tin of cat food?' he says, 'It was so bad I couldn't even smell the wife.'

And it never came out?

'She's always known I don't like the way she smells.'

So the cat is still in there.

'I don't know.'

So take the mattress apart.

'Ahh,' says Dealy…

Ahh *feck'n* what?

'That was a Significant Pause,' says Dealy, 'Yours was a Significant Lack of Integrity.'

Ahh.

'So if we take the mattress apart,' he says, '…then one of three things will happen.'

It will escape.

'Alright, four.'

I await the enumeration…

'Number One. We find that the cat is dead.'

Would you not know by the smell?

'Between the tin of food and the wife that is no certain conclusion,' he says, 'I remain in pursuit of more than a Hypothesis here.'

Would you not have been better engaged in pursuit of the cat?

'That assumes the existence of the cat.'

The Lardy Cake punches the air with wild abandon.

'Number Two. Unless we can establish the existence of the cat, Number One cannot apply.'

So the cat that died of Fear and Ignorance may not be dead?

'It may never have existed at all.'

Then that makes you a liar.

'But only in this Dimension,' says Dealy, 'Number Three. The cat is still in there and is still alive.'

How long ago was this?

'About three years.'

Then I think we can discount this one as probability over possibility.

'I discount nothing,' says Dealy.

And neither does the Co-op up the road …although Tinkers offer kittens on a buy-one-get-three-free basis.

'Number Four.'

This is mine…

'And it's pathetic,' says Dealy, '…to think I would not have noticed the lump in the bed was gone.'

So what finally happened to it?

'I'm ignorant of that,' he says, '…and I was feared to look and find out.'

What about the wife?

'She's still alive,' says Dealy, '…if a little ravaged by Entropy.'

Strike Two

Benigglety is limping around the Ward as I slide through the door unannounced. His back is to me and the huge white gown that almost fits sprouts ginger hair in clumps between the straining ties …and I can see at a glance that Anonymity has eluded him all his life.

The hair at the back of his head is vertical from the pillow in fair imitation of a fire drawn to the chimney. He swings the useless leg around and follows it with the crutch.

'See, McEarly? Takes more'n one blow to strike down a Tinker.'

You're a Proper Man, I say, You should be made an example.

'They say three more weeks,' he says, '…now the gob's working right again.'

The nurse in the corner of the desk looks up at me with a slow shake of the head until Benigglety spots her.

'What you shaking at?' he shouts over, 'I'm well enough to tell you in the dark. You have the one hand warm and the other cold. Do you think I don't know what you and the other girls are up to when you think I'm out of it?'

He leans against me and I'm crushed into the soles of my shoes, 'The blanket baths…' he says in my ear, '…almost worth the stroke.'

On the desk is a pen that scribbles away and a hand above it looking desperate in pink nail varnish.

'If I had my time again,' says Benigglety loudly, 'I might consider the Health Service.'

Doctor? Surgeon? Consultant?

'Nah,' says Benigglety, 'Paying into it. There are benefits here I never before considered. Like the Private Room.'

The pink from the hand is now gracing the Nurse's throat.

'I was brought back to the Ward for the rest.'

Was that a disappointment?

'I insisted,' he says.

I pull out the chair beside the bed to sit in and Benigglety throws his vast frame across it.

'Get on the bed,' he says, 'I've spent enough time in it.'

He stares across at the nurse who stares back then stares at me and I stare across at the nurse who glances at Benigglety then looks away.

I didn't come to interrupt anything, I say.

Benigglety's good hand throws me onto the bed.

'How's Shel?' he says.

Has she not been to see you?

'Not the last week. She says you're the full-time job.'

If she ever does take a job, I say, she'll be very good in the Post Office.

'I heard about Sheary,' says Benigglety, 'The Ward was full of it.'

Dominos, I tell him, Wife-Dog-Sheary. If you say it fast enough it begins to make sense.

'It didn't make sense to him.'

Oh yes it did. ...The Wife with no gall bladder ...the Dog with no lead ...and at the bottom of it all is a Sheary who tells everyone he meets to *feck off* with such regularity that friends can only inhabit the spaces between. You can imagine the size of the sack of coal he was carrying around.

'But I don't understand the cycle clips,' he says, '…for the man had no bike.'

He was Renting, I tell him.

Jonjo Benigglety tries to look me in the eye and one is the ooze of sauce on the ice-cream but the other is still a razor, 'Don't feck *me* about, McEarly. What was he Renting?'

Safety, I tell him.

'From what?'

From Insanity.

…and from the friendless losses and the Hysterectomy they wanted to give him…

'Speaking of which,' he says, 'The Mammy of your Wife was in here the week before. She was very complimentary about you.'

I find that hard to believe.

'True as the hand of that Nurse,' says Benigglety, 'She never mentioned you the once.'

His left hand reaches up for mine and draws me to the chair.

Benigglety, I say.

He shakes his head vehemently.

Jonjo.

'That's better,' he tells me.

Julius, I say.

'McEarly.' he says.

…and I see the tongue is swifter to the shape and in here the pecking order doesn't seem to matter …for a Tinker there can be no Wrong Side to the mattress.

How are you really?

He points to his face. The side that was recovering the day I brought Shel has slipped back again. His right arm is useless against the arm of the chair.

The nurse gets up from the Station and comes over.

'I don't want him getting excited,' she says.

As long as I stay between you I think he'll be fine, I tell her.

She scowls and goes back to the game of FreeCell on her monitor.

'McEarly,' says Benigglety, and beckons me closer, 'Caravan.'

I have seen it, I tell him, A wonderful contrivance of Chromium, Gas and Generators.

…not to mention children …or indeed its former role as Cradle of Civilisation cut ruinously short by the loss of the wife…

His face screws itself to the very crumple of an empty chip wrapper. He lifts his huge frame by the one good arm until he is close by my ear, 'If… I don't… make it… Yours…' he whispers, '…all of it …Furnisha …effertin in it.'

…the caravan is easy …but I wonder if eBay take Children…

There is a clock on the wall with a finger that ticks softly while we wait for well-ness to intrude through the swing doors of drugs and chemicals and the flash of knives with conscience autoclaved from the blade …but most of all for the benefits of Hospital Time.

I ask how he spends the Waiting.

'Sleeping,' says Benigglety, '…and the listening and the watching.'

That sounds remarkably Tinker.

'Aye…' he says. The nurse turns away at his glance. '…and there's no shortage of opportunity in here.'

The chair groans beneath him as he slumps further in.

'Will you bring Shel?'

Now?

'Next time you come,' he says.

Wait a minute, I say.

…three floors down through the tiny glass window panes I see the Fox in the undergrowth by the edge of the drive…

I'll be right back.

The Nurse follows me into the corridor as I leave. She clips the sleeve with her nails and for a moment I think…

'Mr McEarly…' she says.

…the last person to call me Mister was Dealy so the pomposity of it reaches out to grab my soul…

How can I help you? I ask politely.

'Do you know if Mr Benigglety has made any arrangements?'

For what? I say, The Repatriation of the Elgin Marbles?

'Don't be so *feck'n* clever, McEarly,' she says.

I look around the corridor but the *Mister* has fled so fast there's not the echo of a footstep in the ringing air.

'He's due for the Operation tomorrow.'

Which Operation?

…from the size of Benigglety they could have dropped him at Arnhem…

'His Carotid is occluded. He's to have the Stent fitted,' she says, 'The inevitable result of our poor Indigenous Diet.'

Potato …Man's Best Friend.

'A dog is safer,' she says. 'Give my love to Shaughnessy.'

I would …but I can't even afford to give her mine.

'Why go Private?' she says, 'When there's a whole range of benefits open to the Health Service.'

Do you have the small car?

'Not on my wages.'

Then I can't explain the Physiotherapeutic Benevolence of a small cramped back seat.

'Give some thought to Benigglety,' she says.

He would never have fitted.

'Arrangements…' she says.

Don't worry about that, I tell her, He just this moment wrote his Will.

'Do you have the Witness?'

God, I say.

'That's fine,' she says, 'They're used to Him not turning up for The Probate.'

There is an entrance at the side where Ambulances rush and yellow hatch lines are squealed with rubber. The passageway to it is littered with gurneys and the gurneys are littered with people with eyes pleading for a respect no-one including myself has the time for.

I pass along shedding scales of shame into the non-slip glimmer of the flooring.

Shel is head-deep in a bush from where the Main Entrance can be observed when I creep up on her.

...I am six feet away...

'Hello, McEarly,' she says without turning, 'I missed the scent at first. It must be the handwash.'

I hold out my hand...

Shel... come with me.

'No,' she says, 'I have a job to do.'

Shel...

'No.'

Shel ...Hold my hand.

'Why?'

Because if you don't I might think to hit you with it.

'That's alright then,' she says.

Benigglety is sprawled huge across the chair.

'Shel...' he says.

Shel is microscopic in front of him.

'Da...'

I might have to leave, I say, This looks like an emotional situation by which I could easily be overwhelmed.

Shel turns to look at me and then away.

The side-line shifts beneath my feet and I am forced to step back along with it.

The Nurse turns out the green lamp on her desk and the walls pale cream in the pure daylight. Clouds stutter the window and I hope for a Mackerel sky but the Tails of the Mare whip the stratosphere into shivering blue and I am alone in a Ward filled with Waiting where Time ticks slowly and people shuffle through dimensions of Pain and Suffering and the Nurse is down by a cupboard where the door is small and white and filled with envelopes cascading to the floor and one good arm reaches out and crushes Shel to the bosom of Benigglety.

'Da…'

Slender arms reach around Benigglety's neck.

Tears well up in his one good eye and stream to where their skins meet.

'Ingvild.' he says.

Shel pulls away from him.

'Ingvild?'

'Your Ma,' says Benigglety, 'She chose it for you before she died.'

'Call me Ingvild, McEarly,' says Shel, '…and You Are So Dead.'

I let go of her hand by the side of the driveway. She looks up at me …begging the question.

I thought you might want to get back to your job by the bush.

'The job is like Easter,' she says, picking up my loose hand, 'It's a Moveable Feast.'

Three stories up beyond sky-metalled windows in the land of Hospital Time where pale walls wait in silence a green light clicks on and a clock ticks once and by the time it ticks again there is a slip of eye and a drop of jaw and a steady slide of Benigglety's bulk towards the floor.

Mission Belle

Kayla Shaughnessy slams into the bar. I duck behind the pint as she marches up to my table and takes the glass. She places a hand each side of my face and consumes me with a kiss that sucks my eyes down into their sockets while her tongue swims wild and unusual in my mouth.

'Thank you, McEarly.'

…and I'm pink like the salmon and gills pumping…

'Thank you,' she says.

She turns quickly to rush away and at the bar behind her is the Ruby.

'Still renting I see, McEarly,' she says.

I'm Aghast, I say, I have No Idea…

'That's true,' she says, '…and don't get the wrong one this time either. I'm only sitting down because I'm 'shamed to go home and tell Beryl and the Mammy that they were right about you.'

They've always been right about me.

'But do you have to prove it *every* time I come in here?'

It's a very convenient place for the Truth, I tell her, It's somewhere I'm a known quantity.

'I want the Quality, McEarly. I don't mind that there's only so much of it.'

Are you saying that I must relinquish my Option to Purchase on the grounds of insufficiency?

'You don't get out of it that easy, McEarly. You left a Deposit.'

...and the wink of the Mammy that has stayed with me closes on a land of coal-skips and drawn curtains and the deep seafloor warmth of a bed...

'Where's your Fox, McEarly?'

The Ruby's stride is longer than mine ...and her feet more willing on a cool night where the sound of our footsteps is the only pair.

I check the watch the Ruby has bought back from the Landlord as a token of misplaced affection.

She'll be home by now.

'Where's home?'

Where the Heart is.

'Platitude.'

Isn't that the weird Australian thing with a beak like a duck?

She spins me around, 'Looks that way.'

Have you ever kissed a duck?

'The odd frog ...and never a Prince among them.'

A bus is trundling the night street and I recognise the number. I steer our steps to the stop and hold out my hand.

'Where are you taking me, McEarly?'

Wait and see...

'It's dark.'

Don't you think it's marvellous the way the Night does that?

'Where's the moon gone, McEarly?'

I think her skirts are in for the cleaning...

'And I think mine will be too come tomorrow,' says the Ruby, 'What are we looking for?'

The Earth.

'Do you mean the stuff that's filling the front of my sandals?'

No …I mean the Planet of The Fox.

'Not the grit between the toes?'

No.

…and I stop …as the field lays itself out in front of me in shades that are grey but distinct and there's a sudden sharpness of tyre wires and they are completely and utterly avoidable …and beyond them the caravan is an infrared array of muted chrome…

'What's the matter, McEarly.'

Hold my hand, I say, I think I'm becoming Feral.

The caravan door swings open and children pile out into the dark.

Shel rubs her eyes, 'McEarly. I've only just gone off shift.'

Shel …This is Ruby.

I drag the Ruby by the hand until she's beside me.

'We know that, McEarly,' says Shel. She shouts through the doorway, 'Ragnar. Put the light on.'

Inside the caravan a beacon fires in the gas mantle. The glow is green and surreal in the faces ranked by the door.

'Come in,' says Shel.

I wade through the carpet with Ruby at the hand until Shel drags bedding from the couch and we can sit down.

Shel holds out her hand and Ruby takes it gently in hers.

'Hello …Shel,' she says.

'Hello …Ruby,' says Shel.

I sink into the couch with eyes closed …safe as the leaves of a book between percale-bound covers.

'What shall we do with him, Shel,' asks the Ruby.

'I don't know yet,' says Shel, 'I was given him. At least you had a choice.'

…and behind my eyes I hear the Ruby say…

'No …I didn't.'

Benigglety's Brood climb slowly back into the caravan.

'This is Ragnar,' says Shel, '...the twins are Sigrid and Gudrun, then Oleg and Cnut.'

Where's Loki? I ask.

'We're never sure,' says Shel.

'I was up the Hospital with the Mammy yesterday,' says Ruby, 'They say your Da' has another stroke?'

...a book-end shifts and I lean towards the Fox and marvel at how soft a word can belittle so mighty a man...

'McEarly called me in to see him,' says Shel, 'I knew I shouldn't have gone ...not with my reputation.'

...the Fox leans towards me and her inner tubes are filled with the tremors of pumped air...

It was your Da' called you in.

'Da?'

He wanted to show you the love he's hidden in that huge bucket-pump of a heart ...and he wanted the chance to call you Ingvild.

'Ingvild?' says the Ruby.

'McEarly,' says Shel, 'You Are Officially Dead.'

And there goes my chance of ridding Life of its Inheritance...

'Can we have another light on?' says the Ruby.

A generator kicks in outside and light gleams from etched-glass cylinders around the pelmet until we find ourselves awash in a sea of bedding. Sigrid gathers it into a pile by the bay window and we sit looking at each other in the surprised glow.

Ruby glances around the living space, 'How do you all manage?'

'It's a Shift System,' says Sigrid, 'We have a Rota by the door.'

'Do you stick to it?'

'Mostly,' says Shel, 'Unless McEarly gets in the way.'

'Have any of you thought of taking a Job?' asks the Ruby.

…no-one moves yet shadows shy away into the corners…

'A Job?' says Sigrid, 'You mean like…'

'Like Paid Employment,' says the Ruby, 'Like going out at certain times of the day and coming back at others.'

'I never thought of it like that before,' says Sigrid.

'It's a Shift System,' says Ruby, '…but without the distraction of McEarly.'

'How would I find one?' says Sigrid.

'Don't worry about that,' says the Ruby, 'One just found you. I need some help with the Mammy.'

'And you'll pay?'

'There'll be an Allowance for the Caring. I'll have to apply first.'

'Don't give it another thought,' says Sigrid, 'Shel? Get out the box of Benefit Forms.'

She turns to Ruby, 'How many times do you want me to apply?'

'Once will do,' says the Ruby, 'I don't know what kind of Post-Hysterectomy treatment the Mammy would receive in Jail.'

'But I'm a Tinker,' says Sigrid, 'I won't know how to deal with the shame.'

'Look on it as a Mission.'

The pool of light at the Terminus misses the stop by six feet. We stand under the lamp where shadows drop stark across the Ruby. I lift up her face and my tongue inserts itself slowly into each of the darknesses until it finds the salt taste in which it feels at home.

'What are you doing, McEarly?' she says.

I'm the Explorer …amongst the Tastes and Tingles of you where the Wild Things go…

'Does it have to be so wet?'

Is the Source of the Nile so dry?

…or so abundantly fecund of the imagination…

'McEarly?'

What?

'I'm not asking you to stop …just to let me catch up with you once in a while.'

I'm not the runner.

…I'm the swimmer of silver shingles and each nailed on by a single tear…

'I know you're not the runner,' she says, '…but if I could catch up with you …I think I could love you.'

…and if you loved me, Ruby …I think I could love me too…

Welcome to The Shoal

'So the Tantivvy has died down, Julius?'

So it seems …but I'm wary of false silences, I've heard them before.

I settle into the Monday morning seat beside O'Daly and I see at least a third of the puzzle is complete …and what's more …the answers are correct. He catches me looking and smiles. I like to see O'Daly smile. It makes me think of Bank Holidays and the Inconstancy of Luck.

'How are you doing with Dealy?' he says.

Fine. I couldn't afford the New Scientist so I weaned him onto the International Journal of Meteorology.

O'Daly stares out the window beside him.

'At least the Phenomena are more obvious. Was the weaning difficult?'

Not once I pointed out that if his predictions included rain he would have a better than seventy-percent chance of avoiding error.

'How's the Fox?'

Still trying to decide whether or not to eat the Fish.

'And Jonjo?'

He's had a Relapse.

'You mean he's started paying his Taxes?'

There is only so much skin on a man. It's unfair of the Government to take more than he can bear.

'Have you seen the size of him?' says O'Daly, 'I could re-cover a three-piece from one mighty leg.'

But it's the thinness, I say, There's so much Benigglety inside of it that bursting is surely an imminent option.

'I want to thank you, Julius.'

If it's to do with Kayla Shaughnessy I was thanked Saturday night in the bar and it almost cost me a divorce from the woman I have not yet married and I will not let you kiss me this morning because my lips are still sore.

'The woman is a Walking Miracle,' says O'Daly.

Visionary, I say, I recall her Lazarine Attendances with great fondness.

'She came around last Friday night for the completion of the paperwork.'

Paperwork?

'Disclaimers …Declarations of Independence too, I shouldn't wonder. It all looked Kosher.'

So does your Degree.

'But only in Illinois,' he says, 'Whereas she is here.'

Bird In The Hand, I say.

…but Kayla Shaughnessy is good in the bush also…

'I had a Firm Diagnosis on the Saturday Afternoon.'

I am unsurprised.

'I never had such a thorough Examination in my life.'

An Experience to Cherish, I say, When you get back to the College, make a point to steal a red pen with which to Grace the Calendar.

'How long is it since you were thoroughly worked over by a Member of the Medical Profession, Julius?'

…and my immediate thoughts are of the two female Gynaecology Students who beat the sarcasm out of me in a bar in my very first year…

I am wary of comment, I say, on the grounds of Diminished Irresponsibility.

'I have the appointment already made for next Thursday,' says O'Daly, 'If you can take the time, I would like the company.'

Nurse Kayla should be adequate without my assistance.

'No, Julius. To the Hospital.'

To the Hospital? The place so un-Meteorological you have a better than seventy-percent chance of *becoming* an error?

'The Stent, Julius. Nurse Shaughnessy says I need the Stent to be fitted.'

Do they make them that long? I thought they were a small thing that nestled beside the heart.

'They took her word like it was the Gospel, Julius. Her telephone manner was impeccable.'

I have had many the conversation.

…but none so softly erudite as with the Ruby…

'I have something for you,' he says.

My old sock reappears from his pocket and there is a muted ching of spring steel.

'She took them from me and put them in the drawer by the bed. Said I would never need them again.'

I have no desire to kick over your skittles, I tell him, but do you have the idea of the size and dependency of her workload?

'She has signed them all off so she can concentrate on my case.'

Can you cope with that level of concentration?

'It's her idea. She's recovering from a sense of failure, Julius. Spread herself so far that one of her patients died. I think we can help each other.'

Then make sure the rope is only around the waist, I say, What time Thursday?

The evening bus is dreary with people grey-eyed from the Friday at work and I'm glad to see the stop approaching. I start to get up but a hand clamps my shoulder and I'm held firm to the seat. I look around.

Shel?

'No.'

…and at once I can see she's bigger while being the same Shel that nibbles the sleeve in and out of Post Offices and I turn further in the seat…

Gudrun?

'Sigrid,' she says.

…and I nod …for the control of my life has been subverted by the fox yet again…

Her hair is the same as Shel's but modish as if hers has been the right way through hedges. She smiles and I call up a night-whoop from the dark of another dimension.

'Stay on the bus,' she says.

Where are we going?

'To see O'Daly.'

…God! It's the Friday already …and only yesterday he had the Stent fitted against my very promise to accompany him …and in which duty I Failed Miserably…

Is he..?

'He's fine. He's in good hands.'

…Immeasurably so ….Ruinously so in fact…

I could have called home for the better jacket, I say.

'You have a visitor there,' says Sigrid.

Oh.

'What are you doing, Julius?'

O'Daly is in the bed with apple-pie corners and a top sheet folded down across his chest like a transom. I'm staring with fond memory at the curves of Kayla Shaughnessy as she bends to the flecks and spots that dare alight on the cotton.

'Julius?'

Sorry, I say.

'What are you looking for?'

To see if it still has Hilversum on the dial.

'It's Digital now,' says O'Daly, 'You just have to press the right button.'

I'm sorry I'm late. It's a singular capacity I have from the Mammy's side. Of late they're all late.

'Julius …shut up and sit down. I owe you my life and I want to talk to you about it.'

You owe me nothing. The Fish has sole allegiance to The Shoal.

…and his room is just as I imagined …with two exceptions …the neatness is extraordinary …and his socks match…

'Julius …I don't know what I'd have done if you hadn't given me Nurse Shaughnessy's card.'

Shaughnessy casts a wry grimace, 'You'd have died …that's what,' she says.

…and there is something wicked and good about delaying the inevitable …and somewhere in Time and Space I hope this balances out poor Sheary's ballast of Dark Matter without which the Universe of Love would expand forever …with or without cycle clips…

Fraud Brothers, I say, It's in the blood and unquenchable.

'A Question of Degree,' says O'Daly.

Questionable indeed.

'Look here, Julius.'

O'Daly turns back the sheet. Around his left thigh is a large pad of gauze and lint. He peels it back slowly.

Be careful, I say, despite the insistence of the Priest I never got as far as Revelations.

…and now the lint is gone there is a large sticking plaster with bruise spreading rainbows from under…

I thought the Heart was higher up …above the waterline?

'That's just the hole in the ice, Julius.' He taps his chest, 'The Fish are further upstream.'

What did they catch?

'They caught a friend, Julius …and he caught me before I walked off the end of a very short pier.'

'Six months,' says Kayla Shaughnessy.

Such an accurate Diagnosis, I say, should not pass without remark.

'They were impressed, Julius. You should have seen them.'

Yes, I should …and please don't keep reminding me of the fact that I am Calenderically Challenged.

'It was all in the Notes,' says Shaughnessy.

Notes?

…this has the hint of the Black Mail to it…

'Of course I took the Notes,' says Shaughnessy, 'First thing we were taught.'

There is a School?

'There is a College.'

And do they accept volunteer patients?

She looks me up and down with eyes that have seen everything in their stride.

'You could volunteer for the Pathology,' she says.

…and not only am I to the quick I'm now to be down to the bone…

'I had a First in the Nursing,' says Shaughnessy, 'Before I went Private.'

Privacy and Notes are seldom comfortable in the same bed, I say.

She pulls the sheets back over O'Daly's legs and tucks them in again.

'The second thing they taught us was to Study your Subject before Following your Passion.'

…and I think of the times I'd cut out the middle man of that particular argument and by the looks on their faces I am a man readable by expression…

'Correct me if I'm wrong,' says O'Daly, '...but am I reaching the inescapable conclusion that you two have also had the Professional Relationship?'

Psychiatrically speaking, I say, Nurse Shaughnessy is compleat in Counselling by Telephone. We have had many the conversation ...though most of my replies have been incoherent and as such a fitting Testament to her Skill.

'Was that on the card?'

Indelibly, I say.

Sigrid appears in the doorway with two mugs of tea. Shaughnessy takes one for herself and passes the other to O'Daly. Sigrid looks at me and shrugs.

'There were two mugs,' she says.

He must have been expecting company.

'I brought my own,' says Kayla.

'If you don't mind,' says O'Daly, 'I want to talk to Julius alone.'

And here you sit, I tell him, A man cut from the Fabric of Death.

'But not like you, Julius, not cut from the Fabric of Destiny.'

You look well on it, all the same.

...I raise a smile ...for his hair is today a brighter blonde than I have ever seen. His cheeks bloom under the weight of a burgeoning well-ness rare in a man measured so recently in Dog Years...

'The Aquarium,' he says.

And the funny little Uniform with a man inside.

'And the waiting,' says O'Daly.

And the Lifespring Water.

'And the Discovery.'

Ah ...I say, The Discovery.

'I discovered you there, Julius,' he says, 'How come you didn't find yourself?'

The Layers, I tell him, It's all about the Layers. How long do you think it takes to discover a Woman?

'Forty-two years to find just the one,' he says, 'I don't hope to find another at that rate.'

You won't need to if you keep peeling back the Layers.

'What will I find?'

You'll find the Wild Things ...and they'll bring the night-whoop dredged willingly from the lungs ...and you'll find the Silent Spaces so deep dark you can close your eyes and swim in Starlight...

'And the salt?'

There is always salt. Nothing attracts the Cod quite like it.

'How deep is the salt, Julius?'

As deep as you like it to be, I tell him, for women say that only a Man can put it there.

'And how deep is yours?'

Scale deep. Where it ships and glimmers Ruby in her light.

'Then you need to tell her.'

For the once, I tell him, I'm lost for words.

He pushes the folded paper across the bed. The crossword is complete. He taps it with the end of the pen, 'Forty two across ...seven letters... 'Honesty'.'

I scan the puzzle and push it back towards him.

Eighteen down ...eleven letters... 'Trepidation'.

'That doesn't mean you can never tell her,' says O'Daly.

Because I can't deny the call of the Spawning Pool, I tell him, doesn't mean that I relish the upstream journey.

'Scales are only a Layer,' says O'Daly.

They are a Flexible Container, I say, Holding within the Mayhem and keeping out the Ridicule.

'Thirteen across ...eight letters,' he says, ''Claptrap'.'

Is that an Answer or a Comment?

'Neither,' says O'Daly, 'It's a Way of Life.'

And now you have one, I say

'Thanks to you, Julius.'

Though I urge you to the caution in all things Shaughnessy.

'Julius,' he says, 'I love you for loving me but there is something you should know.'

Could you hold on, I say, while I affix my hands firmly over my ears for there are some things a man should never know about a friend.

'Shut up, Julius.'

I have the Clam Affinity, I say.

'Good ...Julius, I'm not a Fool. I know who she is.'

Who? The Queen?

'No ...She's not The Queen.'

You're telling me The Queen is not The Queen? I have my knee bent to an Impostor all these years?

'For God's Sake, Julius. Stop Swimming.'

Then can I hide instead?

'You're already doing it,' says O'Daly, 'I need you to come out.'

I have little left to Admit, I say.

'Only yourself,' he says.

To whom?

'To yourself, Julius. Just to yourself.'

You asked me where the salt was, I say, Deep inside of a man there is a capacity with not even a sieve for the light sprinkling of the grains.

'Then use the shovel on it.'

...I would ...but the handle is Pure Ruby...

I think the Heart may need the Stent, I say, and I can no longer afford the Diagnosis.

'The Diagnosis is no longer available,' he says, 'Especially by Telephone.'

Anything that helps me remain coherent is welcome.

'Julius ...she says she loves me.'

The Holistic Approach can only be good, I say, If a little sudden.

...and his eyes are a-sea with salt-flow as the scales silver his cheeks into a reflection in which I see myself...

'I never had...'

...his voice breaks the way it did after four steep flights and the revelation of my Future...

Surely the Mammy? I say.

'She gave me away at birth, Julius. I've been a Fraud ever since.'

You're not a Fraud, I tell him, You're being repaired under Warranty... like a Monday morning car.

'But it hurts, Julius.'

Belonging can be Such Sweet Sorrow.

...and the scales slip his face until they drip from the gills and I recognise a fellow-fish. I lean forward to plant a kiss on the smooth un-slithered forehead...

Welcome to The Shoal.

Floating a Dead Horse

I'm curled against the back seat of Shaughnessy's car in all too familiar fashion but this time the loneliness sets in instead of the cramp as we pull up outside my flat.

'Stay down, McEarly,' she says.

I'm the Crouch, I say.

'That's a new one,' she says.

Life is nothing if not a Wellspring of Experience.

'Don't milk it,' she says, sliding into the void outside replete with Nurse Kayla Uniform.

I peer over the window's edge. The door to the vestibule has been opened and there's a figure in Orange Tweed waiting by the step. Shaughnessy steps up to meet him and while his attention is inevitably distracted I wind down the window.

He moves aside to let her through but she catches his arm.

'Have you been inside?' she says.

'The door was open,' he says.

'Did you touch anything?'

'I had a drink of water,' he says.

'Oh God,' says Shaughnessy, 'You'd better come back in.'

She pushes him through the door and up the flight of stairs. I slip from the car and follow them. There is a cubbyhole under the stairs with a Trans-Dimensional Wormhole in the ceiling through which the Mice access my kitchen. I sit myself down on a cast-off suitcase to listen…

'Show me where you touched,' says Shaughnessy.

'Just by the sink,' he says.

…and there is the beginning of a tremor to his voice…

'Help me with this,' says Shaughnessy.

'What is it?'

…but I know what it is …It's the roll of 'BioHazard' tape we picked up from the Hospital on the way here. I hear their footsteps above me as it's strung around the kitchen.

'What's the problem?' he says.

'Tell me exactly what you did,' says Shaughnessy.

'Well …I,' he says, 'I touched the taps on the sink.'

'Oh Dear …Then what?'

'Then I used the glass.'

'Oh God,' says Shaughnessy, 'You used his glass?'

'How was I to know?'

'To know what?' says Shaughnessy.

'That he has the …what did you say it was?'

'As far as I recall I didn't,' says Shaughnessy, 'But an outbreak the size of this is Notifiable.'

'To whom?'

'The Authorities,' says Shaughnessy, 'Where did you say you were from?'

'Just across The Border,' he says.

'You'd better make yourself comfortable this side,' says Shaughnessy, 'For you won't be going home anytime soon. Just hold this…'

'What are you doing?' he says.

'I need to check something,' says Shaughnessy, 'Just hold the apron.'

I hear the distinct rustle of starched cloth above my head.

'Just a minute,' says Shaughnessy.

…and the comforting sound of a skirt zip reaches across the Dimensions. His breath blows out like an airlock and I know what he's seeing. I can't understand why they call them suspenders. I never saw anything more uplifting in my life…

'It's alright,' says Shaughnessy …and I hear the zip go back up… 'I have the right underwear. These are impregnated against it.'

'Against what?' he says.

…against me …but not against O'Daly…

'McConaghy's Fever,' says Shaughnessy.

'I never heard of it.'

'You're from Over The Border,' says Shaughnessy, 'This side and you would have had the vaccination immediately at birth.'

'It's not too late?'

'Are you beyond forty?'

'I'm afraid so,' he says.

'Then the Isolation and Palliative Care might be all you can expect,' says Shaughnessy, 'You'll have to make yourself available at The Hospital.'

'What will it do to me?' he says.

'That depends,' says Shaughnessy, 'For it's an old disease that favours the Constant Mutation. First you have to understand your relationship with the origin of it. Over this side it's in the Genes so it no longer has the major impact. It came from a slave ship that dumped its cargo in the harbour at the sight of a Navy Frigate. They tied the chains to a dead horse and threw the lot over the side.'

'That's what happens when you introduce the Death Penalty…' he says, 'It has a habit of calling for the Draconian Measure.'

'It would have made no difference at all,' says Shaughnessy, '…for the horse had been dead so long it floated.'

'And it was the slaves that were infected?'

'They never found out,' says Shaughnessy, '…for it was the Potato Famine and as they swam ashore we ate the lot.'

'And from this you got the Genetic Infection?'

'It was a Genital Infection,' says Shaughnessy, 'I see you have the first symptom already.'

'There are others?'

'Well documented,' says Nurse Kayla, 'The second is imagining yourself in a Sexually Advantageous Position with a member of the Medical Profession ...and the third is a tendency to Prolonged and Uncontrollable Bouts of Sleep.'

'Is it dangerous?' he says.

'Not really,' says Shaughnessy, 'It occurs mostly after dark.'

'What do I do now?' he says.

'Well...' says Shaughnessy, 'You can either slip unnoticed back across The Border ...or present yourself at The Hospital and claim Medical Asylum. Either way steer clear of Public Transport.'

'Won't I spread the Infection if I return home?'

'From this side of The Border,' says Shaughnessy, '...nobody will *give* a feck.'

'You can come out now, McEarly. He's gone.'

...the cubbyhole door is open and the Uniform is proud and starched before my very eyes...

Can't you come inside instead? I say.

...to dispel the loneliness that followed me in here...

Am I not to be allowed back to my own flat?

'McEarly,' says Shaughnessy, 'You've seen the tape.'

I know, I say, but I'm the only BioHazard in there ...and when I'm not in there...

Shaughnessy looks at me in a descending manner, 'Some of us are inoculated against you, McEarly.'

And I thought the whole world was against me ...not just the some of you.

'You have that the wrong way around,' she says, 'For some of us are unfortunate to have the love for you also.'

Then why insist on the rental?

'It's not always the mutual agreement you might suppose …Julius.'

I'm pushed out onto the Hospital forecourt and the car door closed against me.

'Go on in,' says Shaughnessy, 'When I called earlier they said they wanted to discuss Benigglety with you.'

I hope he's alright.

'I hope… No,' says Shaughnessy through the car window, 'I won't say it.'

Tell me, I say, What is it in Life that you hope for?

'That they get more sense out of you than I ever did,' she says. And the arse of her little car flips the speed bumps in a reciprocal fashion.

The nurse comes away from the window overlooking the Car Park.

'Still renting I see, McEarly?'

Oh no. I'm merely a passenger on the Train to Nowhere.

'I hope that's not a return ticket,' she says.

With one foot nailed to the floor by the Deposit, I tell her, it's becoming something of a Circular Route.

Benigglety is a slur across the bed that straightens up as I walk over.

'McEeeaarla!' he says.

'Mr Benigglety…' says the Nurse.

Benigglety's good eye is a spark that ignites the flambeau of hair above. He looks hungrily from one to the other of us.

'…is ready to go Home.'

But is the Home ready for him? I ask.

…for there is bedding where the stand for the drip must be and the thought of a syringe loose amongst the lack of running water, gas and electricity is more than a man should bear…

'That's your problem,' says the Nurse.

I have no room left in the Coffin, I say.

'For what?' she says.

To put another promise in.

'Mr Benigglety has you down as Next of Kin,' she says, '…and as of next week has the self discharge.'

…and if there's a Form for it I have a lot of History I would like to discharge myself of…

Benigglety is more alive than I have seen him for weeks. His head rotates like the crowd at Wimbledon and full half his face is aglow with smile.

'Sign here,' she says, '…and I need an address for the Ambulance.'

He can't come to me, I say, I'm the BioHazard and have a tape to prove it.

'He can't go back to the caravan,' says the Nurse, 'Without the proper care he won't survive.'

The Rules of Chess

'A Tinker's Girl, you say? …and what's *that* doing here?'

…of all the Crises in all of the World the Mammy has to walk into mine …for she winks at me again…

There are tiny teeth nibbling from behind.

'What do you have there, McEarly?' she says.

I pull Shel out from behind me …if only so there's cloth left in the sleeve.

'Ah…' says the Mammy, 'The Fox.'

Shel backs up until she's stood on the tops of my shoes. The hair is a conflagration at my chest and I push her forwards at the shoulder.

'Right,' says the Mammy, 'You can go now, McEarly.' She glances quickly at the Ruby, 'You too.'

Shel turns away with me but the Mammy's hand streaks from the bed to clap her arm.

'Not you, Girl.'

Shel has the look in her eyes of going down for the third time. The Mammy pats the bed beside her.

'I have a job to do,' says Shel.

'Let Ruby do it for now,' says the Mammy.

'But the job…' says Shel.

'For now,' says the Mammy, '…you'll have to do what all capable people do when they need a break.'

'What's that?' says Shel.

'Send in The Clowns.'

I lean on the Dog Bin with an elbow.

How do I compare?

'To what?' says the Ruby.

To all the other men who beat a path to your door?

'That came out wrong, McEarly …they beat it *past* my door.'

And the Appendant Particles?

'At least yours aren't in a second-hand Sainsbury bag,' she says, 'Take me to the Cinema.'

It's early of the Saturday afternoon and the prices will be cheaper.

'I knew you'd find the merit of it if I gave you time,' says the Ruby.

I look up …and at the window is a Fox with the hunt in its eyes and the brush etching steam from the wall of a glass cage.

The back row seats are a starving mouth yawning red and empty across the auditorium but the Ruby will still not have it. We sit three rows in with the draught coming down from the ventilation of the projector room and I wish that a symptomatic dog would curl itself around the shoes so I could attend on the Ruby without the Antarctic undertones.

Her hand strays across to find mine and we sit there twisting fingers while the new Fire Curtain is down.

I stand up in the seat to stare around the cinema.

'Sit down, McEarly,' says the Ruby, 'What on Earth are you doing?'

Earth is *it*, exactly, I tell her, for there isn't a Fox in sight.

'And should there be?'

Why else would a Chicken exist?

'Why would you think you were a Chicken when I know you know you're a Fish,' says the Ruby, '...and a queer one at that?'

Imagine, I say, that you were blind...

...the Ruby closes her eyes...

And that you were deaf...

...silence...

And there isn't a tactile inch of your body...

'Get on with it,' she says, 'I'm imagining.'

Then allow me to explain the Rules of Chess.

'Did anyone ever say you have the look of Clint Eastwood about you?'

What Vintage?

The day is obscenely light for exiting the cinematic womb. It wraps uncomfortably around me and I wish it away for the nights when I rode the dark full six feet from the ground beneath my Da's warm trilby hat and him grinding huge and giant of the strides below.

The Ruby is still thinking.

Am I a 'Make my Day' or a 'Madison County Bridge'?

'Be quiet,' she says.

I squint my eyes until the light narrows into a band of luminescent blue neon.

'I have you now,' says the Ruby, 'You're The Man With No Name.'

...and I smile...

'What are you smiling at, McEarly?'

...because I'm The Man With Two...

The house is silent as we enter. I look around but the Uproar has been and gone and even tidied up after itself.

'What are you doing, McEarly?'

I'm looking for scratches at the door.

'Foxes that size go in and out the window,' she whispers, 'Look at this…'

She takes the reefer from the hook where it hangs sleek as a seal. I fold it back and there's not a trace of the lemon-yellow.

Is it Beryl's?

'No …It's mine …but it's been brushed.'

We creep up the stairs to the Mammy's room and she's full asleep in the bed. She stirs and shuffles in sheets and blankets until out from under the edge of the duvet comes the shade of a sleeping fox.

This is not my Fox, I say.

'Then whose is it?' whispers the Ruby.

…I lean closer for a better look…

This one has straight hair, I tell her, Mine has a style more privet altogether.

Ruby picks up the hairbrush from the bedside table and pushes it into my hand.

'There's your answer.'

I give it her back.

I cannot be doing with disguises, I say.

'Other than your own,' says the Ruby.

'And I have a message for you, McEarly,' says the Mammy …even though she is still of the closed eyes and pebbles of sleep in the mouth…

'Ingvild says …If you wake us up when you get back …You Are So Dead.'

The Ruby prods my walking corpse back down into the kitchen. A flame flickers wild under the kettle and soon I am galvanic with hot tea.

The Ruby looks at me and starts to cry over the waver of a smile.

My own eyes fill and the Ruby shape-shifts in the overflow glimmer until I finally realise the sadness in a Picasso.

'Why are we crying, McEarly?'

Because there is no Law …Moral …Legal …or Scientific against it, I say, This is Life's Last Bastion of Freedom.

'So we do it because we can. Is that what you say?'

No. In the words of a man most famously rooted in the Irish… 'We choose to do these things not because they are Easy …but because they are Hard'.

Return to Zenda

'McEarly?'

Surrounded as I am by three women and a blackthorn hedge the choices of escape are narrower than I once suspected.

Ladies?

…they're an odd crew …every conceivable size and weight forced unwillingly into a triptych…

'Are you waiting for the Ruby?'

I'm inspecting the hedge, I say, It's the time of year for the pruning of blackthorn and the Council can't let it get out of hand.

They look at each other then at me. My fingers are amongst the thorn needles and calculating the puncture of the skin that may be called for.

'She said you were strange.'

She said that …did she?

…and I wonder at you too, Madam …and your five-foot-eleven-in-stocking-feet and hands with fingers that twist this way and that as if made to fit the threads that wrap them every day while you wait for the factory whistle of doom…

'Do you have none of the shame at all, McEarly?'

…and the fat from this one is a proving roll of dough inside the fold of jumper and the look of her face is a signal for the knocking-back and re-shaping of my own features…

There are days I have nothing left but, I tell her.

She harrumphs her arms beneath her bosoms. Ticks of cloth and thread leap the air and follow her contours to blanket the ground.

The third takes a step towards me and the sharpness of the hedge breaks skin. Her eyes study the dandruff on my shoulder. A hand twitches subconsciously to brush it off then slowly lowers to re-join the other at the clasp of a handbag too big for cabin luggage.

Her hat has become a distraction …it fits so close there cannot be hair beneath the tight knit and weave of black wool …I look again …she isn't wearing one.

'She's off the work ill. Don't tell me you didn't know,' she says.

When did this begin?

A glance passes silently between them and I see a relic of the way they spend their days in clamoured silence amongst the vibrant machines where their eyes must speak volumes and their grimaces are the thunderclap of disapprobation.

'Four weeks ago.'

'Just the odd day at first.'

'Said she was waiting for a visitor…'

Well, I say, She has those aplenty.

'She should have said you were stupid, too.'

I make no claim to fame whatsoever, I say.

They meld towards the bus stop and never glance back. My fingers ebb away from the anticipated thorns and enter the pockets. There is a slip of paper. I take it out.

It says…

'Go and see her, *Feck'n Eejit*.'

…and that's a strange name to sign a note with…

The lights are on upstairs at the Mammy's House as I hop off the bus. There is steam on the glass and flickers in the blur.

The door opens and Gudrun/Sigrid is/are studying me as if I'd escaped and slithered my way down the path from the dog bin.

'The Ruby is sick.'

Of what? I ask.

'Of you …probably,' says Sigrid/Gudrun.

She pushes her head around the door frame.

What's the matter?

'How do you manage to do *anything* sensible without Shel?' she says.

I don't know, I tell her.

…but thanks for making me feel the loss …it's a keen wind through a cheap cardigan and ice-riveting to the skin beneath…

Is she not here?

'She's off shift,' says Gudrun/Sigrid, 'Otherwise she'd be firmly attached until five-thirty.'

What happens then?

'I feed her …then Ragnar takes over. It's not seemly for Shel to stand by the pub door for half the night.'

If it's all the same to you, I tell her, I'd like to see the Ruby.

'If you wait there,' she says, 'I'll discuss the matter with my Employer.'

The door is shut against my face and there is frost in the glass and in the air and in the voice that has latterly furthered my conscious sense of loss and displacement.

Ruby comes to the door and I'm glad to see the smile doesn't drop off when she sees it is me.

'We're busy here, McEarly,' she says.

I can come back later.

'No, no, come in. One more won't make a difference.'

She reaches out into the cold of the Saturday late afternoon to take my arm.

'And anyway …I'm glad to see you.'

I slip off the old jacket and smile at the way it nestles successfully against the Ruby's reefer. In the kitchen there is a slip of fox passing the door.

Sigrid?

'Gudrun,' says the Ruby, 'Sigrid is hoovering upstairs.'

Where's mine?

'In the Mammy's room,' she says, 'But there's a problem, McEarly…'

What can I do?

'You can get her to come out.'

She will blossom in her own time. Just give her another four years and she'll…

'McEarly …I can't even get in the door.'

Then how are they fed?

'Shel will only open it a crack.'

And watered?

'The Mammy has a Gazunder,' says the Ruby, '…of Antediluvian proportion.'

Ingvild?

'You Are So Dead,' says the crack of the door.

How can you kill me if you stay in there?

'The Mammy says we'll issue a Fatwa on you.'

Shel?

'Is anybody with you?' says the crack.

I look around and the Ruby shakes her head.

No.

'Is that an Inner Tube, McEarly?'

I'm afraid it is. …full and pumped with the air of necessity.

'See…'

See what?

'You can't even lie to me, McEarly.'

But you can lie to me. Is that the size of it?

'Only when you need me to.'

Then I think The Truth would fit nicely round about now.

'Alright, McEarly,' says a growing gap in the door, 'We're engaged in a Struggle to The Death.'

What about?

'Not about, McEarly,' says a visible two inches and the sound of a skittering wardrobe, 'Over.'

Alright. Over What?

'Over you,' says Shel.

Her arms maypole around me and drag me into the room where the Mammy is sat up in bed with a hardback book beside her.

'It's my fault,' says the Mammy, 'I was reading to her.'

I pick up the book ...The Prisoner of Zenda ...and I'm fastened to the quick by the arms of the Fox ...and glad it wasn't The Man in The Iron Mask.

Ruby, I say, This is madness. You can't possibly agree.

'Then why did you ask?' she says.

I only mooted it to the Table. I never expected to find so willing a Second.

'It's the Mammy. She says it's a fair trade.'

I thought that was Coffee and Bananas.

'Sounds like a reasonable description of the both.'

Where will he sleep?

'In the room by the Mammy's.'

But that's your room.

...and the scene of much of my speculation...

'I have a plan,' she says.

...and that's what I'm afraid of...

Not the Flat, I say, I'm excluded and it has been given over to the sole discretion of the Mice.

'I have only the one life, McEarly,' says the Ruby, '...and I'm not about to waste it refurbishing your flat.'

I thought you were up to the IKEA?

'Look around you, McEarly, the IKEA is up to us.'

The Ambulance is a transitory flash of Battenberg green and yellow. The drip stands and blister packs are stacked behind the hedge while Benigglety is manoeuvred through the door and up the stairs. I look down through the window to where foxes are nibbling them into the house.

Shel?

'Behind you,' she says.

…and the world has a continued resonance that is not altogether uncomfortable…

The Noah Syndrome

The new cabin is a considerably less formal arrangement than the one that …despite my recent promotion …we are still excluded from.

'Can I put a shelf up here, Mr McEarly?' says Dealy.

But that's where the roof leaks.

'It's only temporary.'

The shelf or the leak?

'The rain,' he says, 'The Forecast for the tomorrow is good.'

And the Margin for Error is..?

'I only have the Issue 2,' he says, 'Issue 3 will tell me where to select the best kind of seaweed.'

And the two pine cones over the door?

'Issue 1,' he says, 'Knowledge is the Real Power and Revolutionary to the Daily Life.'

…and to the Wealth also …as each issue self-siphons my disposable income into the growing depression that is Dealy…

'See that cloud,' he says, pointing upwards through the open door, 'A cloud like that means it's going to rain.'

It *is* raining.

'Proof Positive,' he says, 'And a sight better than your seventy percent chance of Accuracy.'

How do you know that?

'Step outside yourself, Mr McEarly. You'll get *feck'n* wet.'

I mean …how can you tell that just because it's the right kind of cloud …it will actually rain?

'It's the height,' he says, 'The lower it is the more chance of the rain.'

How do you measure that?

'Don't know yet,' he says, 'Issue 6 is about the measuring. I may have to splice some planks.'

What about the coffins?

'I could stack them,' he says, '…but the chipboard would never take the strain.'

Why's that?

'Because they're all outside and it's *feck'n* raining.'

Shouldn't we bring them in where it's dry?

'It takes a Brave Man to *feck* with the Forces of Nature,' says Dealy.

Drowning by Lumbers

O'Daly is up from the bed and the caper on the carpet is a joy to the watching eye.

'I can't wait for the Therapy to begin again,' he says.

Is it not yet on the roster?

'Not yet. Kayla says she's keeping me quiet for the while …but I'm fitter now than since I was seventeen,' he says, 'According to the Doc it was a Natural Occlusion. I must have had it all of the life.'

And never the notice of it?

'Of course there was,' he says, 'I just slowed down to below the threshold. But now …look!'

…and the caper begins again…

Slow down, I say, Don't let the Nurse catch you.

'I've been trying to catch *her* the last three days,' he says.

That's a Quality of Nursing, I tell him, Where there's a Can there's invariably a Can't.

'It's not the Nursing I want,' says O'Daly, 'It's the Bosom-Snuggle-Sleepy-Drifting-Post-Coital-Expression of Spent Desire.'

That's a Quality of Womaning, I say, Where you've a Will there's inevitably a Will Not.

'How are you coping with the Tribe, Julius?' he says.

How!, I say.

'And the Peace Pipe?' he says.

A little short on the Tobacco. I may have to resort to chippings and glue.

'Dealy looks well on it.'

It's a diet he can stick to.

'When I'm allowed out, Julius,' says O'Daly, 'Will you take me back to the Aquarium?'

To the Order?

'To the Genus.'

To the Species of which we are Specific?

'To the Family, Julius …now that I have one…'

…and the hands fly to the eyes for there are sardine shimmers at the corners when I see the look on his face…

'A man should never neglect the Family, Julius.'

And when the Family neglects the Man?

'Do you remember the eyes, Julius?' says O'Daly, 'The Hundreds of Watchings and the Thousands of Thinkings inside the silver slivers when you were near the tank?'

You could hear them?

'In their sheer choreography,' he says, 'Every letter of your name spelled out loud.'

Are you fluent in the Cod?

'Have you never noticed,' he says, '…how close Shoal is to Soul?'

And there's me thinking you ready to go solo with the crossword.

'I've had it with the solo,' he says, 'For once I'm the Head of the Fish with a Crew and a Thousand Passengers.'

Set them down carefully, I tell him, for they're all Society's Eggs …and as such can be so easily cracked.

'Julius,' says O'Daly, '…look at me.'

…I look at him and *there's* a seeing worth the seeing. The blonde crest is waved to perfection and the pink of the face is above the scarlet of the lips…

The arms lift up and he spins around on the spot.

'I'm *Silver*,' he says.

Hi Ho.

…and Kayla Shaughnessy is The Lone Ranger…

The step outside is slippery with the loneliness. O'Daly's voice is singing through an open bedroom window in the vain hope that The Rain In Spain will stay Mainly On The Plain. I rest my back against the door and feel the tremors of a waterfall run through it and wait while I pluck up courage to make the leap to the next pool in the ladder.

A small car is emergent with Shaughnessy and behind her is my fox. I hold out my hand and teeth nibble the sleeve.

'McEarly?' says Shaughnessy, resplendent in Uniform.

I smile and move away from the door. The teeth follow.

'Are you alright?' says Shaughnessy.

I will be, I tell her, It's a Family matter.

'And personal?'

No, I say, It's more a matter of subscription …and the willingness of the renewal.

'Stay with us, McEarly,' she says, 'I think you earned a discount.'

But The Shoal, I say.

…and the want in her eyes is a ticket to The Ghost Stream …where each fish swims in concert with the loneliness that once haunted this doorstep…

'Bugger the Shoal,' says Shaughnessy, 'Swim your own stream.'

The teeth nibble my sleeve with unwarranted ferocity.

I have to go, I say.

'Don't forget the way back,' says Shaughnessy.

…and her eyes close as I step away…

Thank you, Shel.

'Don't thank me, McEarly,' she says, 'Part of the Job.'

Take me Home, I say.

'Which one?'

…the one where troubles float like lemon drops a-way above the chimney tops and no-one else will ever find me…

Click your heels, I say, Right now this minute.

'Last time I did that,' says Shel, 'I ended up in Limerick.'

The bus is a sullen trundle through the relics of my change at a fare and a half. We span the breadth of the river with evening eyes as railings rattle the staithes below into a zoetrope of stillness where labour and sweat once flowed along the waters. A last-minute sun pierces to the horizontal quick …forcing us to look away from the present economic desolation.

'McEarly?'

I'm listening, Shel, Just because my eyes are closed doesn't mean I'm not.

'Why is your flat full of fish?'

What fish?

'The paper fish.'

You mean the little silver ones that eat the very paste from the walls?

'No…' says Shel, 'I mean the ones that are drawn on nearly every piece of paper in the flat.'

Those aren't Fish, I say, They're Infinity.

'There's a lot of them,' says Shel.

Well there would be…

'Tell me, McEarly, Is Infinity a big number or a small one?'

Don't look now, I say, but I think it's both.

…and smack in-between is the Loneliest Number in the World…

'I'm sorry, McEarly. Between the Work and the Mammy and Benigglety I can't find the time to go out this week.'

The Ruby has the look upon her of the Lost and Found and not sure which she is. Sigrid/Gudrun is running the hoover upstairs and Gudrun/Sigrid is at the sink elbow-deep in suds and there are no nibbles at the waiting sleeve.

Where's Shel got to?

'She's looking for Loki.'

He's here?

'We think so. McEarly, look at this…'

In the corner of the lounge the sofas have been arranged so that the Mammy and Benigglety are laid at degrees with their heads together. Benigglety is laughing in a strange lop-sided fashion.

'Maaalleeeaarly!' he shouts, 'Guuum 'eeere.'

His good fingers crush mine until all I have left are bad ones and I'm sure the Mammy has shed ten years in a fortnight.

'Mm Maaammy knows Tinkersss Cooode,' he says, '…burrits Suvvern.'

'Does that matter anymore?' says the Mammy.

Benigglety gurgles in the back of his throat, 'Norr a mee.'

…and I'm looking between the pair of them and there's a gleam in their eyes that's trying to register on the brain but it will be unfortunate because it called while I was out …out for the loss of the Ruby and the slither slip slide of tired particles…

The Mammy swings her legs around to sit up.

'There was a time, McEarly,' she says, '…when the French rolled their Brandy barrels into Cork because Cornwall was awash with the Revenue Rats.'

Benigglety's head is nodding fit to burst the recent Stent.

' Ohhh onnn…' he says.

'My Family,' says the Mammy, '…were Kings of Cork.'

Well, I say, somebody had to stopper the bottles.

'McEarly,' she says, '…we were Queens also.'

…so was Bloody Mary…

You mean …you're a Tinker?

'To the Blood,' she says.

Moths gather in the leaves of a darkening hedge …poised for the evening ambush of the lamp …their perfect wings are an open invitation to a moon shorn of skirts in a pale sky fading above the eaves of a fading estate.

There is a man by the dog-bin and I watch how carefully he sheds the steaming plastic package through the slot. He wipes his hands on his trousers and I remember the colour and cloth and hope never to find them in Oxfam. He gathers the dog on a fly lead like a kite grounded in the lack of wind and walks off towards the Park.

I try to put my hand in my pocket in search of bus fare but the sleeve has teeth attached.

'Come back in, McEarly.'

I can't do that, Shel.

'It's Home,' she says.

Home is where the Job is?

The teeth leave the sleeve and my hand fits the trouser pocket and there's the barest rummage of coins in there.

'Try the jacket,' says Shel.

…and under the fingers is the solemn rumble of a ten pound note…

I give it back.

I can't take it, Shel.

She hands it back with an unaccustomed firmness.

'It's yours,' she says.

How does that work?

'It works if you believe in me…'

Are you the Fairy? Will you die if I say No?

'I intend to breed that out of the race,' says Shel.

How are you going to do that?

'Wait and see,' she says.

The bus is clumped with people separated by feigned indifference. The driver checks the note before giving me the change. Once deep in the pocket it brings a disquieting kind of comfort …and four pints will bring the invulnerability that once matched to it becomes the suicidal cocktail.

Do you still have the Jack Russell? I ask.

'No,' says the driver, '…and I will not be drawn on the subject either. Sit near the front.'

The lemon-yellow has gone so I sit behind the little control cabin.

Where is it then?

'He's in the Pet Cemetery,' he says, '…but I don't want to discuss it.'

That's fine.

'Do you know how much that costs?' he says, 'Two Hundred and Forty Five Pounds.'

That's an expensive illness, I say.

'He's not ill, McEarly, …he's *feck'n dead.*'

Wouldn't it have been cheaper to keep it alive?

'It was the Sardines,' he says, '…and I can no longer face them in the sandwich so I've had to stop the partaking of the Friday Drink.'

I thought it wouldn't eat Sardines?

'He wouldn'a,' he says, '…but the wife locked him in the shed and while he was trying to get out the stack of tins fell on him. It would have cost more but John Donald's boy at the Co-op took the Sardine for the coffin.'

I didn't know they made them that small.

'Of course they're small,' he says, 'That's how they get so many in the tin. The coffin was a job on the fiddle from Dealy.'

Has it rained since the Funeral?

'You know it has,' he says, 'It's hardly *feck'n* stopped.'

Then I hope he's used to being let out on his own.

Somehow unconnected with my disconnected pinwheel of thoughts there may be a reason why my fingernails are crammed tight with wood chippings …but the speed at which the sardines swim the lattice of my fingers is so amazing it's all I can do but reach out with both arms to gather them in and stem the tide of loss …and however hard I try they escape the cloth and the bare skin to swim deeper into the mulch in which I find myself…

I push my face into the Monday-Friday smell of damp rotting wood until it fills my eyes and nose and mouth and I reach around to stuff it into my ears but whatever I do the thoughts and memories keep coming.

A hand turns me gently.

'Now then, me lad. Does it hurt anywhere?'

Everywhere…

'Can ye be a bit more specific?'

Both sides.

…and in the flash of the Burglar Alarm there is a glint of Garda badge…

'Both sides of what?'

Of me …Inside and Out.

He turns my face with his hand and I allow this …for the comfort of the contact slows the spiralling bewilderment of my semi-circular canals.

'Did ye pay much for the trousers?' he says.

I think I built a well in Africa.

'Can you remember your name?'

It'll be on a little blue plaque riveted to the bucket.

'Given you're such a smartarse,' he says, 'Ye can stay like that until the Fire Brigade gets here.'

I'm on Fire?

'Not yet,' he says, '…but any more lip and I'll torch ye meself for the pleasure of pissing on ye.'

McEarly… I say.

'Is that the Next of Kin?'

Am I alone?

'Yes.'

Then it must be.

'Is there someone I should call?' he says.

No.

...there are one or two he *can* call ...but in my present condition perhaps none that he should...

Was I drowning?

'I think ye attempted that before ye arrived here,' he says.

Only there's fluid leaking from my very orifice, I say.

'Does it smell like beer?' he says.

Now that you ask...

'No surprise there, then,' says the Garda.

Why are you upside down?

'I'm not,' he says.

...and the canals slip a cog and the world spins itself into my throat and out amongst the chippings...

'That's right, lad,' says the Garda, 'Better out than in.'

I wipe the flecks of woodchip from my lips where they stick to the hand like they do to the boots when Dealy spills the gluepot.

I wouldn't mind, I say, if only the going in wasn't so expensive.

'Who was the carrot top?' he says, 'Took off like a rocket towards town when he saw me arrive.'

He settles on a bag of chippings and checks his watch, 'He was your lookout?'

If he was, I say, he wasn't looking out for me very well.

'About fifteen,' he says, 'Tinker stamped all over him.'

...I try to nod but the yard is pressed so tight against my head it won't move...

Ragnar...

'Are you to be sick again?'

No, I say, That's his name …at least I hope it was him …for in my present state of perpendicularity I can't trust myself with the name of his brother.

'What were you doing?' says the Garda.

The finger traces an arc through the mulch until I hope it points at the new cabin.

Home… I say, *…Home.*

The Garda keys the radio on his lapel.

'Where's that *feck'n* Fire Brigade?' he says, 'Can ye jig 'em up a bit? I'm sat here nursin' *feck'n* E.T.'

'McEarly?'

Ruby, I say, Is that you?

…or are you the illusion that's said to haunt the yard by midnight…

There are teeth nibbling the sleeve and brushing the chippings from my hand.

Shel?

…please say it isn't you in my moment of invulnerability that was temporarily suspended by the goings in of beer…

'You're a mess,' she says.

Both sides.

…and if it wasn't for the scales I could be a public monument to stupidity…

'Look at you, McEarly,' says the Ruby, 'You're a Public Monument to Stupidity.'

I turn my face away from her scorn …and there are the legs of Shaughnessy right before my eyes …and the skirt is lofted and flapping with the movement higher up.

'Look away, McEarly,' she says, 'You can't even afford to window shop.'

She grabs at the Garda, 'Hold him still.'

'The Fire Brigade are coming.' he says, 'I can't lift him. It's a Health and Safety Issue.'

I stare along the length of my body to where stars circle my feet and the moon has clearly been jumped and all the little dogs are laughing out loud while Shaughnessy takes her dressing scissors to the trouser hem that has me spiked to the railing.

Aquarius

'Manage your expectations,' says O'Daly, '...and the situations will manage themselves.'

I expected to get drunk.

'With a tenner a-pocket I would expect that of you myself.'

I've always been the stickler for consistency.

'You never disappoint,' he says, 'Though why you would consider the timberyard Home I can't imagine.'

I owe so much of my Eddication to Dealy.

'How's the head?'

Still attached to the Fish. It's only the join that's painful.

'At least the glue came out of the hair,' he says.

Thanks to Nurse Shaughnessy and her Surgical Spirit.

'It's not confined to the Surgical,' he says ...and a smile lights the beacon of his face... 'I'm back on the Roster. But look at you ...what happened to your sense of de rigeur?'

The clothes are fine, I tell him, In fact they're more comfortable now than most I've had.

'I've seen your picture,' he says, '...and a fine looking man you were too.'

The beard... I say.

'Even with the beard I can clearly see a tie around your neck.'

I have one now.

I lift it from the behind the jacket and let if flop like the dog's tongue…

'Since when were you in the Guards?' he says.

Since I couldn't find a Dog House one …search as I might amongst the Oxfam.

'Well …I intend to do something about you,' says O'Daly, '…and NO doesn't even come close as an answer.'

I run my finger around the neck of my shirt.

'What's that in aid of?' says O'Daly.

The collar is tightening as we speak, I say.

'Only the part where the lead attaches,' he says, 'Come on …we're getting off here.'

Far be it from me to remind you, I say, I promised you the Aquarium.

'I'm ashamed to take you in there,' says O'Daly, 'The scales are so worn out …whatever will the Family think?'

He nudges me along the bus seat. I cling tight to the bar and cover the bell button so he can't push it.

Far be it from me to remind you, I say, but I'm a little short on the money.

O'Daly bursts into sharp laughter beside me …then nudges me clear off the seat and presses the bell.

'Get up, Julius. I can't tell the difference between you and the litter.'

Then take the litter shopping …it'll be cheaper.

His hand reaches out and lifts me to my feet.

'And I'm a fine fellow,' he says, '…offering to give *you* money.'

It's a perfect fit, I say, Can I wear it out of the shop?

'For God's Sake, Julius,' says O'Daly, 'It's a glove. Put it down.'

I thought it had a certain ambience…

'How would you like a certain ambulance?'

Alright…

I drop the glove on the counter and there's another there. A dead match.

Michael Jackson didn't shop here, then? I say.

'He would've if I was paying,' says O'Daly, 'A Lecturers pay doesn't run far beyond necessities.'

None of this is necessary.

'Shut up, Julius.'

He calls over the assistant. She's young and swan-plump and heaves up to me with a measuring tape and bosoms. The tape is slung tight around my neck and it's only the warmth she's sharing that stops me crying for Sheary. Her hair is blonde and full and soft with the scent of almonds. Her breath whispers like a shell. There are tiny white hairs in the weft of her black jumper.

Do you have the dog? I ask.

Her smile is a swift shock of white on pink.

'No,' she says, 'Nor the man either …are you putting in the offer?'

'No, he isn't,' says O'Daly, 'Do you have the measure of him?'

'That I do,' she says.

'Then what is he?' says O'Daly.

'Somewhere in there I'd say he was still fourteen,' she says.

'The neck..?'

She rolls the tape into a careful spiral against the palm of one hand.

'I'd say he has enough of that…'

'The shirt,' says O'Daly, 'What size is the shirt to be?'

She studies my face, 'Familiar…' she says.

'Since when was that a size?' asks O'Daly.

She's in my eyes and there's no stopping at the door for even the wiping of the feet. There is a tremor that starts in the webs between my toes and runs upwards until my legs are an Aeolian quiver in damaged trousers. She snaps the tape loose in one hand and reaches around me under the jacket until her hands meet. There is the nudge of her head against my shoulder and it stays there for a second longer than required while her fingers drop and re-find the tape.

'38,' she says.

Give or take a year …or three.

She puts a hand against my skin, 'White,' she says, 'With *easy* buttons…'

'How about the *easy* payments,' says O'Daly.

She snatches a shirt from the shelf and pushes it into O'Daly's hands, 'You pay over there.'

We turn away but somehow the tape snags my arm.

'It's a cat…' she says.

They're so much safer, I tell her, And more dependable when it comes to the sardine.

'Would you like my number?' she says.

Thanks, I say, but I have it already.

'Dear Jesus,' says O'Daly, 'What do I find inside the Cod? A *feck'n* Shark.'

Do you know they have to keep swimming?

'So that's the reason,' he says, 'I thought it was because you were afraid to stop.'

I am.

'Then why not try it for once?'

And when I die?

'I'll buy you a coffin under the counter from Dealy,' he says.

Then make sure it's from the Tuesday batch or it'll never make the middle of the river.

'The river?'

I fancy a Viking Funeral.

'Where will I get a sail that big?' says O'Daly.

The suits are an early morning river-mist of grey flannel and worsted with stripes like the feathered spill of wind-driven petrol.

Can't I just get another pair of trousers like these?
'With the turn-ups cut adrift by Nurse Shaughnessy?' says O'Daly.
Perhaps without the involuntary adjustment?
'No,' he says, 'It's a suit or nothing. Call it 'Rehabilitation of The Man'.'
Does the Soul go first or after?
'The Soul follows you everywhere,' says O'Daly, 'At the speed of a man on horseback. Remember that when you're running.'
Swimming.
'Horses *feck'n* swim too, Julius. Now get in there and *feck'n* try the *feck'n* suit on.'
But it's grey.
'And I will be soon,' says O'Daly.

'Anything else you fancy?'
A coffee. Decidedly a coffee. I need the caffeine to balance my shame against your expenditure.
'I'm still filling up my side of the scales,' says O'Daly, 'When they start to tip away I'll tell you. I know what you gave up for me.'
Two cycle clips and a card.
'Don't forget the sock,' he says.
And Michael Jackson's sock…
…I look at him flitting amongst the blanket grey of the suits …and the blonde hair and the pinkness of his face are small but happy treasures…
We're even, I tell him.
'I'll tell you when we're even,' he says.
Am I not to be a part of this equation?

'Julius,' he says, 'Life is never quite the mutual agreement you might suppose.'

Then I'll be 3.14159.

'That's Pi,' he says.

Then we'll never be hungry.

'Why?'

Because it's recurring...

The bus drops us on the mean Saturday steps where afternoon light softens against the worn stone. O'Daly pays the tickets and we meander through glass walls of watching eyes until we reach the café. He buys two coffees and we huddle the radiator to drink them ...only this time with sugar because I think the salt level in my blood has peaked.

'I need to understand your situation,' says O'Daly.

I thought it was self-managing?

'Only where there are expectations,' he says, '...and of you I have none.'

But you know who I am.

'Yes,' he says, '...but not what you are.'

I'm a Fish.

'Before I can help you,' he says, 'I need to understand what kind of Fish you are.'

I'm Slick of the Fin, I say, Silver of the Moon Flash ...Quick ...

'...of the Gob,' he says, 'So just answer the questions.'

Is this the Test?

'No,' he says, 'It's the Sociological Experiment. Tell me ...what runs through your veins?'

Sometimes it's the Ice-water, I tell him, Fresh from the Arctic Melt ...and sometimes it's the Steam ...lasered live by the presence of The Ruby.

'What is it now?'

Whatever it is it's laced with iron filings as it passes amongst the Brain Cells.

'What's the term for Torture that's self-inflicted?'

I think it's Mortification …and right now if that sounds too terminal then it somehow fits, I say.

'And is there salt in it?'

Only in the wounds, I tell him, Rubbed there by the Unkind Hand of Fate.

'Then you're the Freshwater?'

There's the argument, I say, for when the tears flow like a sweat of sardines there's a terrible tang to them.

'Then you're the Saltwater.'

Not yet. I think I might be a Salmon who would like to be a Cod.

'Then you'll end up an Old Trout like the rest of us.'

…I pick up the coffee cup to stare at him over the brim so he can't see the teeth from which lies have been known to emanate …his skin is glorious of the flush and the smile is a glow that has a tincture of circulation rushing upstream…

You'll never be an Old Trout, I say.

'Julius,' says O'Daly, 'Thanks to you and that little card I now have the chance to be.'

And to the Spawning Pool?

'To the Pool indeed,' says O'Daly, 'Come on, Julius. It's not too late for either of us.'

Be careful, I say, for whichever route you take to the Pool …don't go past the IKEA. It has the way of forming an attachment.

'Julius,' he says, 'Take a look out the window.'

Beyond the glass behind me is the smallest of foxes…

Is there a back door?

'You would never forgive yourself,' says O'Daly, 'You made me look at my future …now I'm looking at yours.'

Do I have to see it too?

'No,' he says, '...but you've been running backwards for so long that you're bound to trip over it any day now.'

See-Back-Ro-Scope.

'Gesundheit,' says O'Daly.

It was on the back page of an old Superman comic, I tell him, Essential for Boys of an Inquiring and Suspicious Nature.

'Can you still get them?'

Someone may be watching us through one right now.

O'Daly looks around the café, 'Where?'

Round the corner ...behind the hedge ...seeing us directly over the heads of the crowd at a football match.

'Can you imagine that?' he says, 'Forty thousand periscopes descending in simultaneous dismay at the result.'

Where do they go if they win?

'Trust me. They only ever ascend through a misplaced sense of partisan loyalty and hope.'

...I look outside the window and shivers are running through the slender frame enough to set the fire of her hair to flame...

'Will you not buy her some clothes?' says O'Daly.

I would ...I will ...but somehow it feels like Anthropomorphism.

'Do you remember the crush of the hand?' says O'Daly, 'And the Loco Parentis?'

Are you now my Rosetta Stone?

'Someone has to be ...for your whole head is a Hieroglyph.'

Interpret, I say.

'You're a man out of balance,' says O'Daly.

I'll admit to a little swim-bladder damage but forty-eight hours without the beer should clear that up.

'You have the Love,' he says, 'A thing Essential to The Diet ...but the Self Respect is sadly lacking.'

When they pick me from the mulch on a Friday night that's hardly surprising.

'You were only there because of the lack,' he says.

I still had change, I say.

'You can't buy Self Respect from a Bar.'

Can I rent?

'No,' he says, 'You only ever rented the comfort of an illusion.'

…and while the rounded surfaces of Shaughnessy press memories out of the skin of my cheeks, the warm necessities of her percolate the chaos of my mind like bubbles of champagne in the blood and my heart fluctuates with immutable mutuality…

I'm Fragile, I tell him.

'I will lower you by hand,' he says.

If you're the friend at all …why are you doing this?

'For Love.'

Isn't that like working and not getting paid?

'The rewards are boundless.'

Be careful, I say, for you know the speed of which I am capable.

'Yes, Julius,' he says, 'But only in one predictable direction. Away.'

Upstream.

'Will you not learn?' says O'Daly, 'I am the Calm.'

Before the Storm?

'Before …During …and After,' he says, 'I'm the Still Water in which you can laze and twist sunlit reeds around your scales until the fractures heal.'

Do you still have the piece of the newspaper?

O'Daly taps the wallet over his heart with a slow finger.

'Yes …but its old news now.'

Entropic of Capricorn

'You're late again Mr McEarly.'

Dealy is hovering around the gluepot warming his hands.

Is that a problem?

'It's perfectly understandable.'

…I wait for a moment …if only to irritate Dealy whose explanation is caught up behind unevenly blackened teeth like an explosion in a sandbag…

'It's like the train,' he says.

I caught the bus.

'The bus is irrelevant,' says Dealy.

But not the Fare…

'The feck'n Fare is irrelevant too, Mr McEarly.'

Ahh, I say, You must have the Monthly Pass.

'I had a feck'n bike until I had to pawn it,' he says.

The price of second-hand cheese can be volatile, I tell him, It's a cause for endless speculation at the refrigerator door.

'What the *feck* does cheese have to do with it?'

On a Basic Level it's all but irreducible?

'That's old knowledge,' says Dealy, 'Science has made Great Strides while you've been sleepwalking into Obscurity.'

It's not the Journey, I say, so much as the Arriving. The Victorians had it all wrong. Obscurity can be a restful place for a weary head.

A Lardy-Cake arrives spontaneously in the hand. Dealy removes a third of it at one bite and turns away, aiming a kick at the gluepot.

'The bus doesn't know where it's *feck'n* going,' he says.

There's a sign on the front, I say, and usually the driver has at least the glimmer…

'But the train is on the tracks,' says Dealy, '…and as such has no Option.'

Then why does it need a Driver?

'Because the Driver is like the God,' he says.

With the God-like Pension, I say, and Ineffable Terms and Conditions of Employment.

'That's the Politics of Envy,' says Dealy, 'I'm talking here about the Politics of Entropy.'

You mean God is a Democrat? We can vote him out?

'Just like a *feck'n* Atheix,' he says, 'You can't *feck'n* wait to escape into the arms of Chaos.'

I think you'll find that's an Anarchist, I tell him, You remember …the guys with the cape and a bomb and a big hat.

'What's the use of a big hat?' says Dealy.

It keeps the rain off your cape.

'And the bomb?'

Would settle the argument about the cat.

'But what about the Wife?'

All women are Anarchists. They impose order in men's lives just so the frustration of the attempt can destroy any order they may otherwise achieve in their own.

'And how can I tell if the Wife is one?' says Dealy.

Look out for the flag, I tell him.

'The flag?' he says.

…the remains of the Lardy-Cake drop to half mast…

It's Purple and Yellow on a Pink background.

'I never seen one,' says Dealy.

Sure you have, I tell him, They plant it with a fist or a frying pan.

'Dear God!' says Dealy, 'It's a shame they keep it all *feck'n* inside. How's a man to know? If only they would wear the *feck'n* hat.'

When was the last time you went to a Wedding? I ask.

The Infinite Fox

Sunday morning has a scent of Fox seeping in from the landing.

'McEarly?'

I open the door and she slides under my arm replete with plastic shopping bag.

Since when did this become seemly?

'Since I brought the tea and sugar,' says Shel.

And the hot water?

'That too.'

And the mugs?

'They were in the cupboard when you arrived.'

You're certain of this?

'You'd never have bought 'Girl Power' mugs in pink.'

Are they not some kind of Feminist Symbolism?

'Only to women.'

And to men?

'A Reminder.'

Shel shuffles papers into a pile on the small table and all the while looking for numbers on the corners by which to order them.

'McEarly, help me with this.'

What are you trying to do?

'I'm trying to line up the fish.'

Hold them further away, I say, Fish are Chaotic at close quarters. It's only when you step away that patterns fall from the random.

She passes the small sheaf into my hands.

'Then show me the pattern,' she says.

I riffle the pages, working the equation into a remembered shape while Shel sips at the tea. I hand them back.

Here.

'Where?'

I point out a symbol at the top of the first page.

There.

Shel reaches a textbook from the shelf by the disembowelled gas fire and sits flickering the index.

Do you know what effect that book can have on your life? I say.

'I know what effect it had on yours,' says Shel.

And you still want to read it?

'I shall learn from your example,' she says, 'McEarly?'

Hmmm?

'When are you going to take the Biohazard tapes down?'

They're a Warning.

'To who?'

To Women.

'We're born with that one, McEarly,' says Shel, 'Have you got a pencil?'

After two hours and the removal of the Biohazard tapes, fifty-two pages have been annotated, scribbled on, struck through and each stroke replicated in the flesh of my soul. Shel puts them in a neat pile on the small table and sits back. She runs her fingers through the fiery tangle to find where she lost the pencil.

What have you found out? I ask.

'Simple.' she says.

Do you understand it?

'I've been reading your books for three years now.'

That doesn't mean you understand it.

"Simple' doesn't apply to the algorithm …that's unnecessarily complicated …It applies to you.'

Is that a considered opinion or a snap judgement?

'Neither. It means you're wrong.'

Wrong? I've always been wrong …but not usually with mathematics.

'Definitely,' she says.

Show me…

Shel flicks through twenty or so ticked pages until she finds one with a thick black circle inscribed in pencil.

'Here…' she puts a finger on the page, smudging the carbon.

I look where she's pointing but there seems no sense of it.

'This fish,' says Shel, 'What's different about it?'

No matter how I look it seems the same as all the others I've scribbled between the lines.

I can't tell, I say.

'It's you,' she says.

I look again more closely but nothing lifts from the paper to enlighten me.

'It's swimming Upstream,' she says, 'All the others are going with the flow. The next thirty pages are simply your way of attempting to correct this basic error.'

No wonder Life is Hard, I tell her.

'You're a Universal Inconstant,' she says, throwing the pile of papers in the air.

Hey, I shout, Some of those might be valuable.

'If I were you,' says Shel, 'I'd let the hoover choose.'

Do we have the bus fare?

'Only if you promise not to look while I get the money. Go on,' she says, 'Turn around.'

…In the window-glass there is a plume of melting fire that twitches in reflection…

'Alright …you can turn around again,' says Shel, 'Where are we going?'

Do you know what your discovery might mean? I ask.

'Beside the 'simple' bit and the 'wrong' bit?'

Yes.

'No.'

Well I know a man who just might.

Today there are no sunlit sandbars …just a slow, turgid brown where the tide swills upstream against the natural flow of waters and as quickly forgotten as the bus descends the bridge to rattle the speed strips where the junction splits us from the lower town. The houses thicken here but soften …pale buff brickwork in arches set with stone quoins lofted above the street by an elevation of small gardens behind slender iron palisades rusting while we watch for the lack of civic pride.

There is a fox a-nibble at my sleeve and it's a thankful anchor against the revolutions in my head threatening to spin me from the seat.

There's a light in Kayla Shaughnessy's eye even though the one in the hall is off to save on the electricity. She presses the door closed and leans her back against it while Shel and I grow accustomed to the gloom.

Is your man in? I ask.

'No 'Hello, Kayla', McEarly? Fox got your manners too?'

Hello, Kayla. Is your man in?

'He might be.'

It's important.

'You're interrupting his treatment. Is it that important?'

It might be.

'Are you not going to tell me what it is?'

No…

'Come on then, Shel,' says Kayla, 'We know when we're not wanted. Go on up, McEarly, while we make tea.'

Shel shakes my sleeve.

Don't worry, I say, Your name will be firmly etched on the prize.

'Julius!'

O'Daly is in the chair by the window. There is a smattering of mismatched socks on a wire rack clinging bravely to the radiator and a crumple of rug to the floor beside the bed.

One flap of the shirt resides without his trousers.

Is this the worst of times?

'*Au Contraire*,' says O'Daly, 'It's the best of times. If you bring nothing else into my life, there's never the lack of Variety.'

What about the Bosom-Snuggle …and the Sleepy-Drifting-Post-Coital-Expression-of-Spent-Desire you were so desirous of?

'Julius…' he says, 'I have Boldly Gone where I never dreamed possible and stood Aghast on Alien Worlds in Strange New Postures until my heart is content. I have mined and shared reserves of salt so deep…'

Then I'm sorry to interrupt.

'Don't worry,' he says, 'These …are the Continuing Voyages…'

I have the problem, I tell him.

'Just the one?'

Pivotal, I say.

'On what does it revolve?'

On being Wrong.

'Julius! I'm shocked!'

What? That I'm wrong?

'No …that you admitted it.'

I had it pointed out to me.

'You never let that affect you before.'

The sun barrels through the window to strike blonde sparks from his hair. There is a flush beneath that spreads rude as health around his eyes where the grey used to inhabit and the skin is smooth and delicate and I wish he would hide it from the light …and perhaps from me also for I have no such quick fix …no stent to fit the pride …howsoever occluded.

I have been trounced, I say, by an expert of a mere three years study.

'That's because you're the Lazy Dog,' says O'Daly, 'Prime and ready to be jumped over by the Quick Brown Fox.'

How did you know it was Shel?

'Because you're the only one underestimates her.'

How can someone so small bring a whole Theory crashing down?

'It only takes one shoe, Julius.'

She had the both when we came in.

'It's a Symbolic Shoe,' says O'Daly, 'It literally clogs up the works. You've been Sabotaged.'

You know what this means for the last three years of my life?

'Yes, I do,' he says, 'It means that you lived them out to every corner and edge. You should worry more about the previous thirty-two.'

But the fear… I say.

'Only sharpened your awareness,' says O'Daly, 'Kept you on the top shelf of determination.'

But the hiding? Not to mention the running…

'And the crawling and the swimming…'

And the meagreness of Coffins…

'And the life it has given you. If you hadn't noticed, you now have friends …and lovers.'

The one, I say.

He turns away from the sun and I can see the lines that the brightness had bleached from his face.

'Don't underestimate *me*, Julius. I know about you and Kayla. I can understand too.'

O'Daly reaches into a drawer in the cabinet by the bed, 'I found her looking at this…'

He holds out a crumpled fold of newspaper that I recognise. I refuse to take it from him.

'There were tears in her eyes, Julius.'

Not my salt, I tell him.

'Julius,' he says, 'For God's Sake look around you. You spray the salt so far and wide that if you worked for the Council the roads would never freeze.'

That's not true, I tell him, People mine me as if I was the Source Inexhaustible. But I'm not.

'What about Shel?' he says.

I'm a Job. She was a given.

'Have you never been given a Job that you came to love, Julius?'

I once looked after a Goldfish, I tell him, and had it so long I refused to give it back …even though the affection was a little one-sided.

'Then stop swimming along with it. It's time to let it go on alone.'

But what about the Genus …and the Family of which we are both a part?

'The Tide is turning, Julius,' says O'Daly, 'Turning …turning …turning …and I need you to be sturdy of the fin. When was the last time you saw the Ruby?'

Last Tuesday.

'*Last Tuesday*?'

Burned into my heart like a flame of rejection.

'It's not rejection, Julius. It's what other people call Life. Sometimes there's a need to keep your head down while the Devil has the reins.'

But there's a Flurry up there at the Mammy's where a Flurry shouldn't be and I'm finding the partaking of the sport difficult.

'Why's that?'

I don't have the Uniform.

'And which Uniform would you like?'

The one that looks like everyone else's.

'No Flick of the Tail? No Silver of the Scale?'

I can't help what I am …but can what I am look different?

'Look at yourself, Julius.'

…and I do …I look down at the scuffs where shoes should have been and the trouser hem pinned to the leg…

'What about the outfit we bought?'

You bought…

'Did you want no part of it?'

I tried but it wasn't me. I even tried to get the mirror to lie but my own self saw through it. I closed my eyes. I clicked my heels. I looked up …and there I wasn't.

'Where did you expect to be?' says O'Daly, 'Kansas?'

Shel says Limerick is the new Kansas.

'Go home, Julius. Go home and put on the suit.'

It's the Sunday I tell him. People will expect I'm up to the Church.

'Keep the steeple at your back, Julius. That way people will think you've already been and will pay you no mind.'

And then what do I do?

'Go and see the Ruby. She has something for you.'

Are you now the Seer? I ask, It's amazing what increased blood-flow to the heart can do for a man …and when was the last time *you* saw the Ruby?

'A while now,' he says, '…but Kayla was up to the Mammy's last week. She's seeing Benigglety on a Consultancy Basis.'

Who's paying for that?

'You are,' says O'Daly.

'McEarly?'

Shel?

'Why are we going this way?'

Because it's the Sunday.

'And why do you keeping looking over your shoulder?'

For the sake of appearances.

'If you cared for appearances,' says Shel, '…you wouldn't go out dressed like that.'

'Up to the Mammy's now are you, McEarly?'

The driver shuffles small change into the relevant compartments and I consider which one he thinks I am. Shel tugs the sleeve into a seat out of sight of his mirror.

In the window beside me is the reflection of a man. This one has on a suit. He also has a Fox. In the double reflection from the window at the other side there's another and I wonder how many of us are rushing headlong the wrong way into Infinity.

I look down at Shel with her feet swinging clear of the floor and the draught skimming bits of discarded ticket into the corners.

Are you Endemic? I ask.

Her feet stop and she studies them quietly for a second.

'No…' she says, 'Agnostic.'

The Ruby is around me in circles and can barely keep the smirk from her face.

'Is that really you, McEarly?' she says.

I have no way of knowing, I tell her, O'Daly says that clothes maketh the man. I'm not sure what to maketh of anything any longer.

'Did you come with him on the bus, Shel?'

Shel nods.

'With him dressed the like of that?'

Shel nods again.

'I think you need a break,' says the Ruby, 'Go on up. The Mammy has been asking after you.'

I check the sleeve and the row of little black buttons are all tight. It's not much but could be all I have to hang on to on an emotionally bleak Sunday afternoon.

'Are you thinking to take me out?' says the Ruby.

Not particularly …but I think the suit has a mind of its own. If you give it time it may well ask.

'It might be dark by then,' says the Ruby.

I've no time to be responsible for the mind of the suit, I tell her, and right now my own is onerous beyond the bearing.

'Do you think it could develop an attraction to the reefer?' she says.

As long as it doesn't become distracted as we pass the Oxfam window.

The Ruby fingers the lapel. Her skin smoothes the fine nap of the cloth into snail trails of reflected silver-grey. She quickly brushes them clear.

'This one has never seen the Oxfam,' she says.

How can you tell?

'Well …it fits for a start. And the shirt…' She opens the jacket wide to see the trim tapering into the trousers, 'What size is it?'

Familiar, I say, She had the measure of me.

'When did you buy this?'

I didn't.

'Then who did?'

Sir Percy Blakeney.

'You mean O'Daly.'

He's the Master of My Disguise, I tell her, Please be careful with his Secret Identity.

'Is he as careful with yours?'

Indubitably …If I had one that is.

'I would never believe it of you,' says the Ruby, 'Two or three or four maybe.'

I'm a whole Spectrum, I say, The whole Richard Of York …and latterly Giving Battle In Vain.

'And if I spin you fast enough will you come up white?'

I think there might still be grey at the edges.

The Ruby reaches up to touch my hair, 'Only at the temples,' she says.

That's why I never go near them, I tell her, Nor Church nor Chapel. They're a certain sign of age Congregating.

'Distinction …and you could do with some,' she says, 'Come on …let's try the park before they lock the gates.'

And which side shall we be?

The Ruby shrugs her arms into the sleeves of the reefer, 'Tonight I don't care. This place is driving me mad.'

Is it the Benigglety Factor?

'The place has never been so tidy.'

Isn't that good?

'Can't find a thing,' says the Ruby.

The river is a trickle beside our footsteps. The shoes are new and the socks walk up to gather in the space around the toes and may be the reason they were so cheap. The Ruby's arm is through mine and I look around but the Fox is nowhere in sight.

'Don't you feel alone?' says the Ruby.

I have you.

'Without the Fox,' she says.

…I look up to where a new moon shorn of all skirts staggers into visibility through the darkening blue…

I hadn't really thought about it.

'Why do you lie to me, McEarly?'

I wouldn't …but you ask questions to which I have no easy answers.

'Then tell me what you're thinking is on the matter.'

I'm thinking that Foxes are a new experience …sometimes so seemly and sometimes so inexplicably wrong that I feel I ought to correct her.

'Isn't that what Benigglety wanted from you?'

I think he wanted an end to the chastisement.

'You don't correct someone with a hand or a fist, McEarly.'

Not even with Love wrapped tight around it?

'McEarly …did no-one ever tell you that Love is an open hand.'

Then what can it hang onto?

'Not a thing. It's just an offer …nothing more.'

…and the Ruby holds out her hand and there is light enough to follow the work patterns in her skin …the edge of thumb thickened by constant tension with the cloth …the finger tips smooth from twill and denim …and as I watch something spills from the openness of it all and I dash to the catch and find myself caught in the silk of another's touch that I fold my fingers around while hers remain open…

I look into her eyes with the question evident in my own.

'It's an offer, McEarly, …take it or leave it.'

I take her hand and slide it into the pocket of the suit jacket and follow it with my own.

In case of rain, I say.

'Julius,' she says, 'Does it always rain where you are?'

Down by the riverside in the dark of trees there is a whoop and the sound of an upended litter bin.

What about the locks? I say.

'The locks?'

Along the bridge rail.

'They're put there by people afraid,' says the Ruby, 'Afraid of losing the thing they think they have. The real thing needs no lock …it just is.'

What about all the keys?

'Melted down and shipped to China,' she says, 'They come back as Fáilte go hÉirinn ashtrays.'

Each and every one?

'Lock it and Lose it,' says the Ruby.

From the end of the park comes a clang of iron as the gates are firmly closed.

Now I know which side we shall be.

'Does there have to be sides?' says the Ruby.

…her hand is a warmth in my pocket that resonates through the fibres…

Not so long as we stay together.

'Together?'

Whether we leave or stay. It doesn't make a difference as long as we do it together.

'I'm glad the moon is full,' she says, 'It makes the shadows darker under the trees.'

You'll get your coat dirty.

'For once I don't care,' she says.

…and her hair is shook loose from the collar and a descending blue strikes a last glint of steel from it as she pulls me beneath the shelter of a filling chestnut…

'I'm too tired to care …and anyway …this one is Beryl's.'

The gates are locked against us in the night air folding slowly into crispness …and I'm not sure I can lift her over.

'I can climb, McEarly, I'm not so old.'

But …so recently they said you were ill.

'I'm not ill, Julius, I'm fine. Just tired. Help me up the gate.'

I take her foot and boost her to the top and push my hands through the gate as a caution while she climbs down the far side.

She presses her lips through the space between the bars and I kiss them slowly in memory of witching light through dark trees hidden from the shadow of the moon.

Be careful, I say.

'I don't need to be,' she says, 'Not now.'

It's a sure way of extending life, I tell her.

'I already did,' she says.

…against my puzzled expression she kisses me again…

'McEarly,' she says, 'Did your Mammy never buy you a Russian Doll?'

Caravanserai

The Mammy looks fast asleep in the bed with only the wire wool of curls showing above the calm of her face. Shel is on a stool intoning the pages of an old book in a hushed voice.

She raises a finger to her lips for silence.

'Da wants to speak to you,' she whispers.

I step quietly onto the landing to go downstairs and from the bedroom comes the Mammy's whisper... *has he gone yet?* ...and the soft interval of their quiet laughter.

'Maalearly!' says Benigglety ...and holds out his open good hand for me to take.

I study it first ...my own is hesitant in the air of recent revelations. His hand begins to drop and I snatch it quickly.

'Aats 'etter,' he says, and pulls me to the chair beside him, 'Wan a tork a you. Wwoon't tek llong.'

Take your time, I tell him, for I have reason to believe that I am become Infinite.

'Shimple...'

You're the second one today to call me that, I say, Does all your family have this clarity of perception?

'Shimplesss dis,' he says, 'Carrvan ...No goo no more.'

I admit it could do with a clean and a good tidy-up but this house is rampant with Tinkers while a good caravan stands empty.

Benigglety rattles the drip stand beside the couch, 'No Carrvan no good ser mee,' he says, 'Ser mee no good ser carrvan.'

There's always the chance of a full recovery, I say.

'Who yoothink y'are?' he says, '*Feck'n AA*?'

I was thinking Medical…

'Aam *Fecked*,' he says.

I look at you and that's an awful amount of disaster, I tell him, Are you sure they can't just hive off the damaged parts?

'Dammage eer, Maalearly,' he points to his head, 'Dammage eer.'

…and as that's the only human-sized part of him I am drawn unwillingly towards agreement…

'Ccaan't go baack,' he says, 'Memba? …memba a zed at ospitall?'

But that was your Will, I tell him, It can't be your Last Testament until you're gone.

…his good hand takes the front of my jacket and the fingers curl into it taking the tie …the shirt …and even the small turning hairs. I feel them tear from the skin…

'Dere's nuff one o' us beeein *Feck'ed*, Maalearly. Dooan mek it twoo.'

I'm Immortal now, I tell him, so I could be persuaded on the idea of that.

'Memba thing, Maalearly,' he says, 'Onny immorrral while yer alive.'

What about the Stent? I ask.

'Wooan giv me *me* baack.'

His hand releases me into the chair and I sit to watch the tear form in his good eye.

'Losss too mush,' he says, 'Tooo mush.'

He turns his face away and the conflagration of his hair is no more than an ember quiet and twinkling in the grate.

'Carrvann,' he says quietly, 'Shoours…'

He rolls over until the bed groans beneath him.

I pull up the cover to his shoulder and touch the skin with an inadvertent finger …and stop …because coursing through me comes all the Tinkerness trapped inside this huge frame with no longer the outlet …and no longer the deliverance of Fear that crowned him King.

'Memba thing,' says Benigglety, 'I know oo yaarr.'

So who am I?, I say.

'Eivver foool,' he says, 'Or mos' 'oness man in cnu …cnu …p'raps wurll.'

So which is it to be?

'Shuury's still ou',' says Benigglety, 'Now *feck off.*'

Shel? Why isn't the chrome shiny?

'It will be,' she says.

Where's the key?

'It's unlocked.'

Is that secure?

'The caravan's always been like that,' she says, 'Da wouldn't give us keys in case we lost them.'

Who else knows that?

'Everybody.'

…and I think of a King deposed on a bed of tears…

Then don't lock it when we leave, I say.

'Why not?' she says.

…and I can't tell her …not while he still has the glimpse of Immortality.

Give me a hand here, Shel?

We drag loose bedding out through the door and throw it over a line stretched to the gutter from a pylon thirty feet away. Shel opens the roof light and air sweeps in the door and through the internal spaces taking with it the dust we have raised. The space left behind is impressive.

I never dreamed it was so big in here.

'Or so empty...' Shel is visibly astounded by the lack of occupancy, 'I never seen it like this before...'

She pulls out a sliding panel from beside the bay window and shuffles it into place on runners. She fills the space with side cushions until it makes a raft of bed wide enough to sail the Sargasso. She looks up at me with a shy sort of half-smile.

'I was born there,' she says.

And isn't that the Marvel?

'And there's where my mother died.'

I thought that was up the Hospital ...the one with the insufficiency of blood.

'It began right there,' she says.

And so did you, I tell her.

'Tell me something, McEarly, Why does it feel like I was born running?'

Maybe that's what Foxes do, I say, I feel like I was born swimming.

'Does that make us a pair?' she says.

A Fox and A Fish?

'Unlikely as that sounds?'

It doesn't sound safe...

'It can be,' says Shel, 'As long as you remember who eats who.'

Fire Alarm

Kayla?

'Hello, Julius. You see …I can remember *my* manners.'

…I look around the doorframe but the landing is clear…

Where's my Fox?

'Outside …servicing my car.'

What?

'Who do you think has kept the Benigglety truck going the last three years?'

I thought it was so scared it just kept running.

'Like you …you mean?'

Kayla Shaughnessy lifts my hand from the door and closes it. She leans her back against it and turns the key. She lifts a knee and the skirt rides upwards six inches.

'I want your complete attention,' she says.

Couldn't you have telephoned?

'You're cut off,' says Kayla.

She puts a finger against my chest to push me back into the sitting room where the absence of loose paper has become remarkable.

'Am I in the right flat?'

If you're not, I'm not, I say, but the key fitted.

'So I hear,' she says, 'And I want to know what you're going to do about it.'

About what?

'About the deposit you left.'

Do I need to start wearing a tin-foil hat? I ask.

'Only if it stops your thoughts getting out and infecting everyone else's, why?'

I was hoping it would be a protection from the lightning …which now seems to have struck twice already.

'Twice?'

Well, I say, First the Ruby and now…

'Now what?' she says, 'Oh no …you can't think …Jeezus McEarly!'

Julius.

'Jeezus Julius.'

What am I supposed to think, I say, You come in here with your finger and your back against the door and the look so deep in your eyes…

'Julius …back up a bit.'

…I take hold of her finger and lift it from my chest. It falls beside her and I dare a step forward…

Do you deny that there are days when I see love behind these eyes of yours?

'I don't deny that, Julius.'

Even while you hold the whole balance of O'Daly in your hand?

'Even then.'

Don't you feel ashamed about that?

'Only in my choice of men.'

What's wrong with O'Daly?

'O'Daly? Absolutely nothing at all. He's a Paragon and I love him dearly.'

I see…

'Sit down, Julius,' she says, 'I'm here in Official Capacity.'

Without Uniform? How am I to take this seriously?

Kayla sits at the edge of the sofa. Her calves cross and thighs push willingly at the cloth of her skirt. Her blouse is a fragile container for the memories I am trying desperately to dispel.

'I'm Officially a Woman, Julius …in case you hadn't noticed.

Then I am obliged to say that your Uniform is Impeccable.

'I want to know what your intentions are,' she says.

Thanks to Shel, I tell her, I now have to revisit the last thirty-two pages of an equation.

'The Ruby,' she says, 'If I have to drag you around by the neck I'm going to get you to talk about Ruby.'

What would you like me to say?

'The deposit you left …you understand what that means?'

That's why I need the equation.

'What planet are you on, Julius?'

The one that insists on a balance of further payments.

'Well,' says Kayla, 'At the moment it's only a deposit.'

You mean I can return it to the shop?

'I mean that …with my help …Ruby can return it to the shop. If that's what you both wish.'

And what does the Ruby think?

'The poor fool wants to know what you think.'

But is that what she wants to do?

'No, Julius, it isn't. This is so close to her heart that to pull it away might inflict the fatal blow.'

The Ruby said that?

'Not in so many words,' says Kayla, 'Trust my judgement in this, Julius.'

She crosses her legs and the red shoe slips to hang from the end of her toes and her credentials are beyond dispute.

'What are you thinking?' she says.

I'm wondering how much of me has to be cut off before the telephone stops ringing.

'That's not the telephone,' says Kayla, 'That's the Fire Alarm. If you don't move you're going to get burned, McEarly.'

…and through the kitchen window comes the sound of a small engine firing up. The throttle blips briefly before the exhaust settles into a remarkably even pattern …and in that note is all the resolution I need…

Will it be a Fox? I say.

'It has every chance,' says Kayla, 'The Grandmammy is a Tinker.'

I rummage in the trouser pocket for change but there is none.

'What are you looking for, McEarly?'

Will you give me a lift in your little car? I ask.

'Only if you sit in the front,' she says, 'Where to?'

The IKEA …It's a while since I read the catalogue.

The Parsimony Tree

'You can find enough money to get drunk on,' says the Ruby.

That doesn't take an awful amount, I say …and I try to tell her that no matter how fast I run away from nefarious purposes the money for them always seems to follow me.

'Then try hanging on to some of it,' she says, 'We're going to need it when I have to stop work.'

I don't know what to say, I tell her, Money has an infinitely variable way of sliding that I can't seem to calculate.

'You could start by trying to hang on to this,' she says.

Out of her handbag she takes my watch.

That was a needless extravagance, I say.

'I cleared your debt, Julius,' says the Ruby, 'Now try and stay out of it …please?'

'First things First,' say O'Daly.

I don't know, I say, What does come first?

'Well …it isn't the Child,' he says, 'It's the Preparation.'

Is it expensive?

'Not all of it,' he says, 'There are things you can bank for free.'

Like what?

'Like several good night's sleep.'

Beside that...

'For free?'

Yes.

'Nothing much. This could be the most expensive time of your life, Julius.'

Do I have time to Prepare for the Preparation?

'A few weeks at most,' says O'Daly, '...and they so quickly fly.'

You sound like a man overflowing with Experience, I tell him, Are you sure there are not more secrets to you than I may suppose?

'All my experience was gained at the Polytechnic, Julius. Do you suppose Sociology Students spend long on their Thesis?'

Can they spell their name right?

'With help,' he says, 'So what do you suppose they do with all that spare energy?'

There was none of the spare on the Mathematics Course, I say.

'And there you have it,' he says, 'Just one of the many advantages of a Prophylactic Education.'

I could ask for a raise at the timberyard.

'He'll give you a plank to stand on ...unless you agree to him sacking Dealy.'

I can't do that ...I have too much sympathy for Mrs Dealy.

'You don't know the woman.'

I don't need to.

'Then what do you propose?'

I might have something I could sell?

...and O'Daly erupts with volcanic gusts of laughter. I look around and if the café hadn't been empty we would have been the subject of multiple glares...

'And what is it you have that has more than curiosity value?' he says.

I have this.

I take a slip of paper from my wallet and smooth it on the table between us. He spins it around with his finger to study it.

'It's out of date,' he says.

Perhaps they will bow to a little educated persuasion?

'I sincerely doubt it, Julius. I know exactly what it's worth and I'll pay you for it now.'

You will? That's an awful amount of money…

He takes a pound coin from his pocket and slaps it on the table…

'That's exactly what it's worth …and I have another coin for the other one that you have…'

The other one?

'I know you, Julius, You wouldn't have bought just the one. You wouldn't have run away without checking first.'

Can I have that address in Illinois? I say.

'No, you can't,' says O'Daly, 'You have the scent of Revocation about you.'

Not true, I tell him, I want to see if they would add layers to your Degree.

'Like an NVQ?'

Like an Onion.

'There's little difference,' he says.

I fold the slip of paper into my pocket and slide the coin back across the café table. The Aquarium is closing and while I wasn't looking someone has barred the door leading back into the tanks. The exit door to the outside has been propped ajar and the temperature is lowering. Through the glass pane is a glimpse of Fox.

'Why don't you ask her in?' says O'Daly.

She's Feral, I say.

'So?'

So I don't want to Domesticate her.

'Why ever not?'

Have you ever seen a tiger in a cage in a zoo? Somehow there's a freedom…

'In what?' says O'Daly, 'In standing out there freezing your nuts off?'

In choosing to.

'Look at the child,' he says.

I turn in my chair to look around the room.

'No,' says O'Daly, '…and there you have it. I mean the one outside …and take that look of shock off your face for I know you've never seen her as a child …but that's what she is.'

Are all children Feral?

'Of course they are,' he says, 'That's why we spend twenty years knocking it out of them. Why on earth do you think we have schools?'

Is that wise?

'Not in the least,' says O'Daly, 'It's about Revenge …not Wisdom.'

Revenge for what?

'For daring to be Feral …and for daring to remind you that you were Feral yourself once before the System battered it out of you.'

Then I'm right, I tell him, in allowing her to keep away from it.

'There are advantages to the System, too,' says O'Daly.

Such as?

'The tiger cage has free heating.'

Is that all?

'It's not an inconsiderable consideration,' he says, 'It supplements a Lecturers Income to the point where it's considerably cheaper to go to work than stop at home.'

Even keeping in mind the Shaughnessy Factor?

'I suspect she's never had to pay a heating bill,' he says, 'The woman is a Generator of Great Steams. The most of which seem to find their way out of my ears.'

Perhaps I can borrow.

'Where from?'

I can try the Bank…

'Ha!' says O'Daly, '…and what good would that do you? Can you climb a tree?'

It's a while since I tried, I tell him, though the Beryl's coat now has a fine imprint.

'First things Banks do,' he says, '…is dig a big hole. Then they entice people to throw their money into it.'

But I want some out …not in…

'Then they put down roots and soak up all the goodwill there might be in that money to grow such a huge, solid trunk that they forget whose money was fertilising it in the first place.'

So I have to climb the tree?

'No,' says O'Daly, 'It's the wrong time of year. You can't get money from a Bank in Autumn.'

Why not?

'The leaves are falling …and the leaves are the illusion that they have something to offer that you might need. Unless …of course …you really need it.'

What if I go in Summer?

'You can't,' says O'Daly, 'You can't get in the Door.'

I don't have a viable door either, I tell him, least of all not a Tinker-proof one.

'Do you recall the door at the Bank by the park? The big brown one with all the panels and brass?'

I do, I tell him, Dark as Dark.

'Do you not think it looks like a wardrobe?'

It might, I say, if I squint.

'And what's in back of a wardrobe?'

Nothing if it's mine …with the sole exception of a grey suit.

'Narnia,' says O'Daly, 'And what did the kids find in Narnia? Winter.'

With little furry animals…

'No Foxes?'

Hard to tell …they turn white as the snow.

'Have you ever asked a Bank Manager for money?' says O'Daly, '*They* do that, too.'

Judas's Chariot

The Ruby's front door is closed and there's so little of the to-ing and fro-ing I feel like a cloud the wind has forgotten. Upstairs has a rumble of hoovers at the landing and laughter from the Mammy's bedroom.

Shel has discovered Great and Good Humour at the Library in the town but wouldn't go in until the Mammy told her she was raiding it.

I open the door because there's movement beyond the frost of glass and find Kayla Shaughnessy circling out by the dog bin.

'Julius,' she says, 'I need your help with O'Daly.'

I thought you'd become a Mutual Society, I tell her, I haven't heard from the either of you in weeks.

'Do you ever have to protect yourself, Julius? From yourself …I mean.'

I don't know anyone else worth the effort, I tell her.

'Then you'll know why I haven't been,' she says.

I wonder …does O'Daly know this?

'Of course he does,' she says, 'but since you gave him the card he loves you even more than I do.'

I don't know how I can help any, I say, I can only jump one brush at a time and I think I'm committed on that score.

'And rightly so,' says Kayla, '…but I need help to get O'Daly committed.'

Isn't that a bit drastic? The last time I saw him he…

'Committed to Living,' says Kayla.

But I thought he was back on the Roster?

'There's more to Life than being on the Roster, Julius …like eating and paying the rent.'

Does he not get the pay for being sick?

'He's no longer on the sick,' says Kayla, 'He's been signed off the last five weeks and the College will not pay him the money.'

Have you thought of…?

'If you're going to ask if I thought of going back to work myself, then I have to say he wouldn't let me even if I wanted to.'

I look around the street and there's no car.

Have you come on the bus? I say.

'I sold the car.'

…and the memories of the cramped smell of plastic leather and torn stitching?

'There was nothing else for it.'

…and the little chrome handle with the spindle at the end that caught my trouser leg to wind down the window to let out the steam and let in the cold wind of reality?

'We've eaten from it the last three weeks and now it's all gone.'

Have you taken him to the Aquarium?

'He won't go with me, Julius. He says only you understand the language of The Shoal.'

Will he ride the bus?

'He says that Jesus gave him back his heart so he could devote it to me. I can't go anywhere.'

You have him tied to the chair today?

'He's tied himself to it.'

Have you tried one that moves?

I don't know what to try any more, Julius. I'm frightened that he's gone Religious on me.'

Have you never heard of Judas's Chariot? I say.

Benigglety… Can I have the borrow of your wheelchair?

'Zuzz ziss 'ave a glim o' silva 'bout it?' he says.

No, I tell him, it has the glint of friendship.

'Bee carefu',' he says, 'I seeen 'at leav men wivv emmty pockits.'

And empty hearts?

'On'y weigh' in S'leshtal Bal'nce,' he says, 'Down 'ere a man 'as t'eat.'

Do you like sardines, I ask, even if the tins are out of date?

He swings his good arm in a slow arc, 'I 'ad Fishh like you a breakfffas', Maleearly. Memba that.'

'You're not bringing that *feck'n contraption* on the bus,' says the driver.

It's for the Disabled, I tell him, It's your duty to carry it.

'That's fine,' he says, 'But it's empty.'

And what if I sit in it?

'You're not *feck'n* disabled, McEarly. It wouldn't be right.'

Do you still have the Sardine, I ask.

'Only the three-quarters of it,' he says, 'John Donald's boy brought it back. Said he was sick of it.'

Let me on and I'll take it off your hands.

'What will I get for it?'

Relief, I tell him, and a fine pair of spring-steel trouser clips.

'How did you know?' he says.

About what?

'About the hole in the bus floor,' he says, 'It blows from the brake pedal and up the trouser leg.'

Then you'll only need the one, I suggest.

'Listen, Mc …*feck'n* …Early. With negotiations at such a delicate stage this is no time to be withdrawing the half of your offer. It's the whole pair or nothing.'

Deal?

'Deal.'

He reaches out a hand to shake mine and without thinking I loosen the watch.

'How will you get them home?' he says.

I point to the chair.

'Oh, no,' he says, 'The deal is for the one journey, then that chair becomes strictly for the disabled again.'

But if I put the Sardines in it...

'They're Fish,' he says.

But they have no eyes, I tell him, without my help they have no idea how to get home.

'Then that'll be one pound twenty for you,' he says.

Oh no, I tell him. Carers travel free.

'The chair's *feck'n* empty, McEarly.'

It holds a fine but as yet unfulfilled promise, I say.

'There's no weight to your promises, McEarly.'

Then think of the saving in diesel, I tell him.

I prop the chair outside Kayla's flat and think to take off a wheel but then remember that I know where all the Tinkers are. O'Daly is a tied fixture in a seat by the window with the blind up and the sash wide to the world.

'I saw you coming down from the bus,' he says, 'Have you seen Kayla?'

He cranes his neck around where I'm stood untying the rope so he can glance along the path.

I left her checking out the Ruby.

'How is the little gem?'

The gem is fine, I say, though I'm a little worried about the setting.

'Surely not,' says O'Daly, 'With Tinkers in place you'll at least know where everything is.'

With the Solitary Exception of Myself, I tell him.

'You have a problem, Julius? The feet are cooling this close to the water?'

I want to swim in it, I say, not walk on it.

'And this is the Sum of their Expectations?'

Cogito Ergo…

'Is that a fact?' he says.

The Ruby is now so many weeks in, I tell him, that we talk as if it were present already. We whisper around the house. Sometimes I think only Benigglety touches the floor.

O'Daly sits upright in the chair to look behind me, 'Where's the Fox?'

She said this was the Suicide Mission and they're always best done alone.

'Why the chair, Julius?'

It's not a chair, I tell him.

'I saw it with my own eyes,' he says.

Then you failed to recognise it as a Wheeled Contrivance of Tinker Origin.

'Then why does it have IHS stuck to the side?'

So I can find it again in the car park, I tell him, In the absence of an aerial and Ping-Pong ball how would I get you home again?

'Julius, I'm afraid I don't want to go out.'

You only lack the willingness I tell him, I have all other means of motivation.

'No,' says O'Daly, 'It's the 'afraid' bit. I'm afraid to go out. I want to be here when Kayla comes home.'

That's not a problem, I say, Kayla says I'm to take you out of yourself for a while. So if we leave the one of you here and the other comes to the Aquarium with me, then we kill both dimensions with one stone.'

'The Aquarium?' says O'Daly, 'Why didn't you say?'

I think I just did…

'To the Genus?'

To the Family…
'To the Species?'
To the Shoal…
'Wagons Ho!' says O'Daly.

'You're not coming on here with that *feck'n contraption* again, McEarly.'
We have a deal, I say.
'Had one,' says the Driver, '…anyway …I know he's not *feck'n* disabled. He's too intelligent.'
Isn't that a thoughtless and pre-emptive statement? I enquire.
'Leave this to me,' says O'Daly, 'This negotiation requires a Degree in Thoughtless and Pre-emptive Statements.'

Can you not just reach down and turn the little wheel with your hand? I say, The legs are tired.
'It's only another mile,' says O'Daly, 'That's practically no distance at all.'
It was the previous four that have come to be a problem…
'Julius,' says O'Daly, 'When did you come to be so inconsequential?'
Do you remember when Art Nouveau sashayed provocatively into Art Deco?
'No.'
Well, I say, it was about then…

'The steps, Julius, Mind the steps.'
If you would consent to get out of the chair it may help.
'I'm afraid, Julius.'
Of what indeed? It's only four steps.
'Of dislocation,' he says, 'Back home there is another of myself balanced precariously by the window with no notion of the stresses I might imply from this great distance.'
Will he be happy watching for Kayla?

'Only when he sees her…'

And when he sees her?

'He will know she's not gone back to work.'

Is that what this is all about? I say.

'I want to see if she stays, Julius.'

Under what circumstances?

'Under the absence of money,' he says.

Do you not trust her?

'Oh, Julius, I do, I do. I trust her implicitly, but I have lost my trust in my trust of myself. Life has changed for me, Julius. When I thought I was dying I knew what I was. But what am I now? What have I become, indeed?'

I tip him out of the chair and he takes the four steps at a rumble then glares at me from where he is propped by the wall.

I entrust you with the Finest of Jewels, I tell him, and this is how you treat her?

'Julius…?'

Fraud… I tell him, and unless you have the Entrance Money I shall not allow you to re-join the Shoal.

The wheelchair will not fit between the tanks unless I fold it so O'Daly is forced to limp behind me. We pass among warm tropical lagoons, our thoughts afloat and bobbing like coco-de-mer until we find the place where the deep Atlantic reaches out to us with its penetrative filigree cold.

Wet your lips, I tell him.

'What?'

Wet your lips. Come on man. Lick.

I push his face against the glass until he sticks there.

Now you're a Limpet, I say, Stick around until I get back.

When I return from the toilet he is pressed to the glass and the shoal are gathered a short breath away. Their eyes are glassy and black and in the reflection so are his.

There is a movement ...subtle within his clothes ...of swimming.

I pull him clear.

The coffee in our cups is formless black velvet with a white rim... the perfect mirror of O'Daly's eyes that stare blankly across the table. I move my cup and the image is broken.

'Julius...' he says.

What?

'Julius ...they are...'

They are what?

'No,' he says, '...they are.'

They are what?

He turns to me ...and the black dissolves into the smoky-blue perspective of eyes that once worshipped the religion of the morning crossword.

'They are,' he says, 'They just ...*are.*'

And you?

'I am,' he says ...and the edges of his lips feather into a smile. He straightens in the chair, 'No, Julius ...I *am.*'

And what are you? I ask.

'Not what I once was,' he says, 'They...'

The Shoal giveth, I say, and now the Shoal taketh away.

'But what was it they gave me?'

Fear, I tell him.

'But why, when it hurts so much? I thought that...'

A man who has never been afraid has never experienced the returning Joy of Certainty.

'I've always been afraid,' says O'Daly.

Aha, I say, that's only the fear of being rumbled.

'But that's endemic in my Profession. Supposition and half-truths are stock-in-trade.'

Can you not teach them to search beneath the bullshit for an Undiscovered Value?

'If I did,' he says, 'the Government would find a way to tax it.'

Then maybe Tinkers are Magi amongst us.

'Do you think Balthazar paid VAT?'

I don't know the rate on Frankincense and Myrrh, but Gold is Exempt.

'Julius,' he says, '…take me home. I have several reparations to make.'

Are you strong enough for that?

'Tears aren't heavy,' he says.

But it takes a strong man to cry.

'I didn't mean *my* tears,' he says, 'I have a flood to stem.'

Will you need the Chariot?

'No, Julius.' He stands straight from the seat, 'Never again.'

I drag the folded wheelchair behind us through dim spaces between tanks. At the exit I lift it over the disability-friendly threshold.

O'Daly grabs my arm.

'Julius. I have to know.'

His eyes are a volume waiting to be filled with sagacity only I seem able to instil.

'What was it the Shoal took away?'

The Fear of Fear, I tell him, A real undiscovered value. How does it feel?

'Frightening,' he says.

'You're not getting on here with that *feck'n contraption* again, McEarly.'

O'Daly draws himself up to his full height of five feet six inches, 'Leave this to me,' he says.

…and that's fine …I need the fresh air …and it's his turn to push.

Outfinity

I haven't been in the flat for weeks but there's something going on here. For one… there's no dust on the stairs …For two …all the papers I left scattered across the living room are in order, except for four carefully arranged A4 leaves on the coffee table …For three …the Fox is sitting on my settee with the broadest grin I've ever seen.

I look all around her carefully…

'What are you doing, McEarly?'

I'm looking to see where the disappearing starts. Is it at the tail end or the Cheshire end?

'That's no cheesy grin,' says Shel, 'This is my look of overwhelming superiority.'

And the justification for that is?

She points to the four sheets on the coffee table. I pick them up and recognise my own notation.

And?

'And …there's your error,' she says.

Who said I was wrong?

'I did,' says Shel, 'Do you remember the little fish that was swimming the wrong way?'

I can't help but remember it. We're related.

'That's where it began,' she says.

I read through the papers quickly. There are scrawled notes in the margin by a hand I don't recognise but the argument follows through as far as I can tell.

I remember this, I tell her, there wasn't a flaw in it that I could find …and heaven knows I looked hard for one.

'When you turned that little fish around,' says Shel, '…you invented the concept of *Out*finity.'

How big is that, I ask?

'Outfinite,' she says, 'That's the error. Your conclusive argument begins at the last symbol on the fourth page. Look…'

She takes the sheets from me and spreads them on the table …the pencil in her hand lately wedged in her hair. She points out the reverse progression across the page until it begins to intuit in that special place I have kept locked and silent for the last three years and nine months.

As I read, figures writhe and flow from symbolic to actual, bending Dealy's space to a mathematically rigid will. I sit down beside her.

Shel …do you understand what this means?

'I do,' she says.

How do you know all this?

'I read your books, remember?'

I know, I say, but without explanation…?

'I'm a Tinker,' says Shel, 'We have an explanation for everything.'

Even the chickens that go missing in the night?

'Especially the chickens,' she says, 'So it's a good job you're a Fish.'

So what do we do about it?

'You could try it out.'

…I recoil from the thought…

I think I've ruptured enough Dimensions for one lifetime, I tell her, I don't think I have the heart for another.

'You could give it away.'

And make a liar out of more people? I don't think so.

…I'm pacing around the flat, a feat impossible until this tiny fox discovered the carpet that treads with such unfamiliarity under my feet…

'What's the matter?' she says.

Alright …Miss-Explanation-for-Everything, I say, tell me why it worked the first time.

'Perhaps it didn't,' she says.

But it did. I *know* it did.

I reach into the jacket for the slip of paper inside the wallet but resist the urge to take it out. I pat the cloth over it.

I have the proof.

'Every Proof is merely a Hypothesis,' she says, '…until a better one comes along.'

Who plagiarised that?

'You did,' she says, '…on the inside flap of the dust jacket of your first book.'

You read *me*?

'The Library's not *just* a bundle of laughs,' says Shel.

That doesn't explain how it works both ways.

'It doesn't,' …and at the look of consternation that inhabits my face she says, 'Trust me on this. I'm Precocious.'

I need to work this through.

'Sleep on it,' she says, '…and by the way…'

She glances at my watch on her wrist.

'Ruby will be here in an hour. I made up the bed for her. I'm off now looking after the Mammy so don't let her come home the night. She needs the rest.'

The Ruby arrives while I'm still scratching away with the pencil.

'What are you at?' she says.

I think I slipped the walls of another dimension, I say, but everything else still seems normal.

'You've never been that, McEarly.'

I push the pencil aside and throw the papers across the room.

Thank you Ruby, that was all the proof I needed.

'For what?'

…to understand that whatever transpired across those papers led me through countless Dimensions until I found you here…

That I'm in love with you.

'You're a good man for the saying of it, Julius McEarly. But is there anything else in your repertoire?'

It seems we have a bed…

'And is there a Tinker under it?'

I expect not …but maybe Dealy's cat…

'Will there be a Tinker outside the door? Or up changing shifts in the middle of the night?'

We exist in a Tinker-Free zone.

'Is that possible?' says the Ruby, all the while slipping off my jacket and draping it across her own shoulders.

Proximity is the only Law that Tinkers obey, I tell her, If anything's going begging there will be a Tinker close by.

'Do I have to beg you, now, McEarly,' says the Ruby, unfastening my shirt buttons.

I come cheap, I say.

'You always did,' she says.

…the belt is loose from the trousers and there's the sound of a zip I daren't even look down to watch…

'But not too early, I hope,' says the Ruby.

I pull away from her before she can dial in from that God-forgive-me number…

Just look at you, I say.

I hold her at arms length. Her belly swells between us with such enormous proportion that there seems no way around or even under it.

She reaches into my open shirt to grab the short hairs that it's a wonder I have any left of and drags me to the bedroom.

'Tell me a thing, McEarly. Did you never put away the cutlery for your Mammy?'

Only of a Sunday, I say, She made me polish them as punishment of not taking her up to the Church.

The Ruby turns around so her back is pressed against me. I fold my hands around her to caress the bump.

'Do you remember,' she says, 'the way the little spoons used to nestle one into the other?'

The jacket slips from her shoulder in what I can only describe as indecent haste. My fingers are shaking so much I can't find the buttons of her flimsy. Her hand reaches up to caress mine and we stand …silent and waiting …until slowly my breathing returns to normal and the fingers become sensory organs that deliver her to me in ways that over the last few months I'd almost forgotten.

I slide my hands into her blouse and she is heavy inside them …palpable and ready …nipples erect with a willingness I've not encountered before…

I fill my mouth with her hair and suck gently on the teasing strands.

This is too late, I say.

'No, it isn't, Julius,' says the Ruby, 'It's me that's too late.'

For what?

'By about two weeks, the Doctor said.'

Then this is absolutely wrong, I tell her, I can't allow you any harm.

'No Julius, this is absolutely right. There's nothing like sex to set the hormones shifting things loose…' she arches her back against me and begins to purr, '…and if you take away your hands I'll never speak to you again.'

I spring elastic free from hidden catches and take the soft culled freshness of her skin against mine. She falls gently under the gravity that transpires generations of us into Family, Genus and Species. My hands slowly caress the dome of her belly. There is unevenness here. A shadow-shape of head, arm and leg. Something moves inside of her and my fingers follow the tremor until passes.

'McEarly?' she says.

Hmmm?

'The bed...'

I kick off my shoes and stand on the sock toes to pull them off. My trousers slide over narrow hips until they pool on the floor. The Ruby turns around and slips the shirt from my shoulders and allows it to drop.

I look down and all I see are creases ...and every crease elicits a memory of the action that put it there as if the days of my outfinite life have been scattered about our feet ...and how unremarkable they are become...

The Ruby slides out of the skirt while I fumble the remaining buttons of the flimsy. They fall together as she looks up at me. I gaze down into her eyes and in a reflection I see the things that are hers cover mine with a layer of bright silver.

Are you the Fish? I say.

'Did you think you were the only one, Julius?'

Crème de la Crem

I'm awake and it's past three a.m. I know this because the 24/7 over the road turns out the sign above the door to save on the electric when there's no-one left to beckon. My legs are warm and wet and the Ruby is nestled snug to me. I sit up, suddenly ashamed. This is a thing I haven't done since I was seventeen. How could my sleeping mind betray me this way, especially with the Ruby …and especially when I've had no beer?

The Ruby stirs at my wakefulness and turns over.

'What is it Julius?'

Don't ask, I say.

'I just did.'

She sits up suddenly, 'Julius. Is your telephone still working?'

Working?

…my three a.m. mind spins a while…

I think so, I tell her, but as wonderful as it was I don't think we should start over just yet.

'The telephone, Julius. For the Hospital?'

The Hospital?

'Are you the McEcho, now,' she says, 'It's the waters…'

I know …I'm sorry …but it's been a long time since I…

'They're *my* waters, Julius.'

Oh …Dear God, Mammy and Jonjo …What do you need?

'Do you have the Yellow Pages?'

Yes I do …somewhere…

'Then find yourself a plumber …but meanwhile get me some transport to the Hospital.'

Transport…

'Kayla?'

She sold the car …Benigglety's wheelchair?

'Are you so ready to die, McEarly?'

And this is how I come to be banging on a door three streets away and apologising to neighbours hanging out of open sashes while from the Dealy household there is not the peep.

Eventually the sash slides up and Mrs Dealy says, 'Is that you, McEarly?'

It is indeed, Mrs Dealy, I say politely, I wonder …can I borrow that wonderful husband of yours to help with an emergency I appear to be having?

'You look fine to me,' she says, '…apart from being a little dishevelled …but that could be the lamplight although, from what Mr Dealy says about you, I think I can discount that as mere hypothesis.'

My brain takes a futile leap into the darkness to ask, Did you ever find the cat?

'In all Probability,' she says, 'I never had one.'

Dealy, I say, we need to take at least three of these coffins out of the van to make room.

Dealy looks around the sky, which is lightening in the east in a very repetitive fashion.

'It might rain,' he says, 'I can't leave them out on the drive. They'll disintegrate.'

Who made them? I ask.

'I did,' he says.

Then have you not got a tarpaulin?

'There's one at the timberyard,' he says, 'We can go round that way. I have a key for emergencies.'

I didn't know you needed a key, I say, I can find any number without.

'Get in, *Mr McEarly*,' says Dealy …and off we lurch.

At the timberyard I open the gate and Dealy drives straight in. I open the van doors and single-handedly drag out the coffins to stack them under the shelter.

'Put one back in,' says Dealy, 'The floor in back of there is awful hard.'

I pick out one with a slick of black velvet and push it back in.

'Oh no, McEarly, I'm not getting in that thing.'

But it's an emergency, I tell her, The Devil Drives when Needs Must.

'And what was wrong with my driving?' says Dealy.

Nothing, I say, nothing at all …but I need a hand here.

'Then why didn't you say? Ruby? …the man wants a hand …will you see to it while I hang on to the handbrake?'

It's the Ruby I need a hand with, I tell him, get your arse around here.

'Alright, alright,' he says, 'Anyone would think it was an emergency.'

'McEarly,' says the Ruby, 'There's such a strong smell of pigs.'

Don't worry, I tell her, Once he's done helping you into the coffin I'll make sure he sits in the front. I can open a window then.

'It's not him, Julius. It's the coffin. What on earth do you do with them?'

Dealy says it's a form of recycling.

'Whatever it is, I'm not travelling to the hospital like this. Besides, it's too tight. Why can't I sit in the front?'

There are only two seats.

'I only want the one.'

Can you drive?

'No?'

Then Dealy must have the seat, for I have the other and I can't drive either.

'We're just trying to keep you secure,' says Dealy, 'for if I have to do my Best Emergency Driving there might some small amount of jostling.'

Are you practised? I say.

'Never caught at the Border yet,' says Dealy.

Ruby …Ruby My Love …there might be something in what he says.

'There might,' she says, 'but for the life of me I don't know what it is. Okay. I'll give it a go before the contractions start.'

'That might be a good time to fit yourself into the coffin,' says Dealy.

'It won't make me smaller,' says the Ruby, grinding her teeth at him, 'Just harder to deal with…'

'Sorry, Pal. You're at the wrong door. Deliveries are around back.'

Is this the place where Ambulances bring sick people?

'See the big sign up there that says …Hospital?'

I do. Then this is the right place.

'It means you can't deliver a coffin here,' says Security Man, 'I told you. They go around the back.'

'But this one's full,' says Dealy, 'It has a bona fide occupant.'

Security Man drags me by the arm to where the sign is in full and plain sight.

'Read that again,' he says, 'If this was the right place it would say 'Crematorium' …and we only take empties. It's *our* job to fill them. So go around the back.'

From inside the van the muffled sound of the Ruby rises to penetrate the metal.

'Come on,' says Dealy, starting the engine, 'Let's go around the back.'

The Delivery door is fast tight and in darkness. There is a bell push beside it with a halo of light around the button.

I open the van door and the Ruby's voice emerges into the early morning air.

'McEarly. What on earth are we doing? Don't you realise I'm having a baby?'

I do, I tell her, it's taken nine months but now I think I've achieved a full understanding.

'Then do something,' she says.

Like what?

'Like *push the feck'n button*,' she says.

'You're early,' says Man in a Brown Smock.

*Mc*Early, I tell him.

'I know who you are,' he says, 'but not what you're doing here at this time of a morning.'

We have a delivery, I say, a very important one. You could say it's something of an emergency.

'You'd better bring it in then.'

Dealy and me grab the handles at either side. I offer a quick prayer to Saint Epoxy of Resin and lift. The coffin slides off onto the rollers that have been ushered up to the van. Once inside, the shutter comes down behind us. Brown Smock Man switches on a very penetrative overhead light. The Ruby closes her eyes against it.

Brown Smock leans over the casket.

'Excellent work,' he says, 'Haven't seen such natural colour in years. Do you know what fluid they used? Last time I saw work of this calibre it was John Donald's boy that did it, but he lost his touch when he went to the Co-op.'

The Ruby's hand springs loose to grab him by the throat, 'I haven't lost mine. Just get me to Delivery …Now.'

He wasn't going to be much help anyway, I say to Dealy, push him out of the way and pull that trolley over.

'Get me out of here, McEarly, this INSTANT!' says the Ruby.

It's no good you shouting in Capital Letters, I tell her, Dealy and I can't lift you out on our own without hurting you.

'How much longer am I going to be in here?' she says, 'for every minute will take a year to erase from your memory. Oh God …I'm contracting!'

'I hope it isn't the measles,' says Dealy, 'It's a very unfortunate disease for those of the pregnant disposition.'

I grab the end of the trolley and push it out into the corridor.

Keep your eyes shut, I say.

…but I don't say it's because everyone is standing aside to genuflect with great solemnity…

I think the traffic is thinning here, I tell her, we may pick up a little speed.

We follow the racing line conveniently painted in precise stripes along the floor.

Dealy bangs through into Maternity.

'We have an emergency here,' he shouts.

The room is empty. He turns around and there is a wild look in his eyes that usually pre-empts a visit to the gluepot.

'Where is everybody?'

'Sleeping,' says the nurse from under the desk, 'Or at least we were.'

'I have an emergency,' says Dealy.

Hold on a minute, I say, if this is anyone's emergency it's mine. You can't go around claiming other people's emergencies. It's not Patriotic.

'Never seen an emergency in a coffin,' says the nurse, 'Time's usually the last thing on *their* mind.'

'But not on mine,' says the Ruby, 'Can you get shot of the fools and get me out of this?'

The nurse walks slowly around the coffin, 'I'm not sure how,' she says, 'It looks a bit snug in there.'

The Ruby looks up at me. Her eyes carry a strange message that I don't have time or enough of the sleep to care to unravel.

'Any more good ideas, McEarly?' she says.

I tap the coffin side with a knuckle.

Dealy? I say, …you're sure this is one of yours?

'Yes, why?' he says.

Then is there anywhere we can soak it with water?

'We have a wet room along the corridor.'

That should do it.

'McEarly,' says the Ruby as the coffin slowly fills with warm water, 'What do you think I am, a Fish?'

…and you didn't think you were the only one, my love, did you?

O'Daly sits beside me. His head is in his hands and the sleep only slowly rubbed from his eyes.

'Why is the Waiting Room full of Tinkers?' he says.

Because being outside wasn't an option, I tell him, Security Man didn't know which way to turn first. In here they're something of a collective.

'Like the Co-op,' he says.

Without the trolleys and the little wire baskets.

'But with the red hair.'

Each one *in flagrante.*

'Where's Jonjo, The Modern Prometheus?'

At home with the Mammy.

'Are they safe left alone together?'

He has a bucket of cold water by the bed to throw over her in case of emergency.

'Why did you send for me if it hasn't happened yet?' he says.

…and it's hard to say that I couldn't think of anyone else I wanted to share this experience with more than himself …for his ego is still fragile …and I think I prefer him that way…

The Universe is expanding, I say, don't you want to be in at the birth of a star?

'I would,' he says, 'but I can't handle the vacuum. Waiting in Waiting Rooms sucks the very air from your lungs. Every cough and wheeze and shuffle appears from the silence like a new menu in a telephone call centre.'

Just keep pressing 1, I tell him, and Kayla says you've had the cold a week now. It'll soon be gone.

'Talking of gone,' he says, 'Where's the Fox?'

I glance down at the jacket sleeve and what I wouldn't give right now for the reassurance of those little nibbling teeth…

She's in with the Ruby. Kayla's there too.

'Then why are you not in there also?'

At this stage of the proceedings, I say, you're no longer the Father… you're the Culprit.

There is a suddenness of Nurse at the door, 'McEarly,' she says, 'You'd better come with me…'

I can tell by her face that this is more than just advice.

She closes the door on a Waiting Room of willing ears and escorts me along the corridor. We stop and she says, 'There's a complication.'

I never thought giving birth was easy, I say.

'You have a daughter, McEarly.'

I'm not prejudiced, I tell her, The days of Dowry are long gone…

'McEarly,' she says, 'You're babbling. Shut up and listen.'

I lean against the wall to stifle the rushing stream of thoughts …and it's hard and unforgiving in pale greens and cream where it contrasts vividly with the trousers I put on in a rush…

'It's the bleeding,' she says, 'That's why we didn't call you in before. The child is fine.'

And the Ruby?

'I don't know,' she says, 'We have the measure of it now but she's lost too much blood.'

Give her more, I say, this is no time for procrastination.

'We don't have it,' says the Nurse, 'It's awful rare.'

I pull up my sleeve to bare my arm…

Here, I say, there's a good eight pints …take it all.

'No, McEarly, it'll be the wrong type. You've less chance of a blood match with hers than winning the Lottery.'

Can I see her?

'Yes …but be quiet and don't excite her. She's tired and I don't want you pushing her over the edge. There's enough with her *arriving* here in a coffin.'

The Ruby is pale. Her eyes are closed and I've never seen so little fire in the facets of my Jewel. Kayla is beside the bed with a look of desperation confirmed by the wringing of hands …the Fox is standing patiently by the end of the bed …if she is worried I can't tell by her face …but no one looks at me as I enter.

Is she asleep?

The Nurse whispers, 'Yes.'

Then what can I do?

'You can hold this,' she says.

…and from a cot by the bed she lifts a large, wrapped bundle to cradle upon my arms …and I almost drop her …she's so heavy…

I look down and the tiniest of faces wrinkles up at me. Her eyes are open and as God is with me they are laughing. I push back the blanket and red hair springs like a fire loose against my fingers. I look up at the Nurse.

She's so big, I say.

'Tinker through and through,' she says, 'A real fighter.'

And my Ruby?

She shakes her head, 'I'm not sure.'

Am I to have only the one Jewel in my Life?, I say, What does a man have to do?

'He has to find me three pints of AB Rhesus negative for a start…'

There are nibbles at the sleeve.

Careful, I say, I have the precious load on board here.

The Fox holds up her thumb, 'Test me,' she says.

The Ruby is asleep so I creep silently through the door.

'Goodbye, McEarly,' she whispers.

Oh no, My Love, I say, *Au Revoir* for sure.

The nurse is back behind the desk of her station as I approach. The question must be scrolling my face like the neon letters.

'She's fine,' she says, 'Just a little sleepy. Would you like to see her?'

Shel?

Shel is curled up on the bed. I slip into the chair beside her. The walls are cream and the light shows no pity. Beneath the blanket there is so little of the Fox she looks like a kite folded and forgotten …the skin where it shows is so pale.

Shel?

Teeth reach from the bed to nibble at my sleeve and the reassurance is a torrent against the tide of the day's direction

…until suddenly they leave and withdraw into the tangle of strings and sheets and loneliness.

Shel?

The tangle draws into a galactic spiral with whirls of white gown spraying off into the waiting æther …and is this the nursery where stars are born unforgiving of the darkness that birthed them?

Shel?

She unwinds and splays herself across the bed. There is a hint of smile pushing through against the encroaching sleep.

Shel?

Teeth snap at the button on my sleeve …worrying the frail cotton thread from which she has me suspended. They close around and snatch it clear. The galaxy of relief whirls around me with the button like the black hole at its heart.

Shel? …will you be alright? I say.

'Ingvild…' she says, through sloped eyes and a mouth filled with the burrs of sleep.

'My name …is Ingvild. Call me Shel again, McEarly, and You Are So Dead.'

The Bus to Valhalla

'I'm sorry,' says O'Daly, 'I did my best, but the umbrella-wielding and the threats a-swash like the tip of a rapier were more than I could bear.'

The Beryl *is* her sister.

I reassure him that what he did was above and beyond the gift of the Shoal.

'All the same,' he says, 'Bad News has a mark upon it, whatever shape it comes in.'

It has to come, I say, for once it sets foot it becomes inevitable. It was only a matter of time.

'What was that old Dylan song?' he says.

Knocking on Heaven's Door?

'No, I was thinking more like 'The Times they are a-Changing.'

…and he always did have the edge on me for optimism…

The coffee in our cups is now cold as the tanks in the next room. The pair of us have stood side by side by against the glass walls, absorbed in the blackness of honest and feral eyes, lost in the sway of an eternal motion that passes through our lives with as little regard as an aberrant neutrino.

I'd buy you another, I say, but the pocket is temporarily embarrassed.

'It's the only bit of you that ever is,' says O'Daly, '...but not yet. There's someone I want you to meet.'

He glances at Kayla's old fob watch pinned upside down to his shirt front, 'Five minutes or so...'

I open my mouth and offer the gape to him.

Can you see the hook in there? Or is it to be the net, drawn ever circumstantially tighter around me?

'You're not caught, Julius. Five minutes is what you have left if you feel the need to keep on running.'

Swimming.

'Swimming ...Running ...' he says, 'It's all about showing your tail-end.'

Does it have a red light? I say.

'God Forbid it should be coming at me,' he says, 'You now have the four minutes to make your usual exit.'

I peer through the door to where the Shoal swims with unerring certainty.

How many are coming?

'Just the one.'

Then I'll stay if you will.

'Why?'

I peer again through the door and catch sight of a thousand fins refracting in the glass.

There's safety in numbers.

I close my eyes as a tray with three coffees slides onto the table beside me. Holding them firmly closed against the tide I smell the familiar scent of wrack-fed sheep in the damp wool of a bright orange Harris Tweed.

'It's raining,' he says.

'Remarkable...' says O'Daly.

'Julian?' he says.

Hello, Professor Montague.

'That's a little formal. Especially for you,' he says.

Alright, I say, What are you doing here, Monty?

'Isn't that obvious?'

Nothing is obvious to a man with his eyes shut.

'Then open them,' says Monty.

That might let the day in, I say, and you along with it.

He starts up from the table but O'Daly clamps his arm.

'I don't think he meant to offend you.'

'He didn't,' says Monty, 'I'm going back for the sugar.'

'Will you not even look at me, Julian?'

No, I will not.

…but my eyes have traitoriously opened and his kindly old face is settling once more into familiarity…

'You look well,' he says.

For a man with little sleep, I reply.

'You never had much sleep,' says Monty, 'Leastways not at night. Lectures were a different matter…'

'He attended Lectures?' says O'Daly, eyes wide with wonder.

'No, Michael,' says Monty, 'He gave them. Insofar as he could stay awake long enough.'

O'Daly leans his elbows to the table, 'Tell me more,' he says.

I drag the watch on his shirtfront.

No time, I say, we have a Funeral to attend.

'Would you mind,' says Monty, 'If I came along with you?'

'Why not,' says O'Daly.

…and I can see in his eyes that he's hanging tight to the tail of this once and future story…

You can't, I tell him.

'Why not?' he says.

It wouldn't be …seemly.

…because I can't find the courage to explain to him that Dimensions only ever co-exist and can never mingle …and that two sides of the same coin should never meet except back to back from where they are unable to make a perceptive observation …and that's how they might be better kept …with the existence of each reliant on being denied the knowledge of the other…

'Where is it?' he says.

On the Water, I tell him.

'Julian, there are two banks to a river,' he says, 'You can stand one and I can stand the other. I would have no wish to reduce your solemnity in this occasion.'

Do you have another suit?

'Yes, I do,' he says.

Then wear this one, I say, the other is like to be so loud they'll hear it in Limerick.

The south bank of the meadow is awash with flame-red hair. Tinkers gather in droves behind the rushes and barbed wire. The big old oak is hamstrung with ponies of all shapes, colours and sizes.

My back has been pummelled, my hand crushed beyond recognition, as we wait for Dealy.

'It's so unfair,' says the Ruby, 'He never got to see her.'

I reach into the carrycot and lift the bonnet covering the incandescent rage of my daughter's hair. Her eyes are still laughing at me.

It's not too late, I say.

'How can you say that,' says Ruby, 'I'm not showing the child to a corpse. She's at such an impressionable age.'

Just hold a mirror in front of her, I say, That'll do it.

Dealy's van trundles through the meadow past a caravan moored like a chromium barge in a sea of unkempt green. On his roof rack is the special illicit coffin he's spent all weekend making. It has a pointed prow and stern and a figurehead that

Dealy said was to be a Dragon but with the sun in my eyes more closely resembles a cat.

O'Daly comes to stand beside me, squinting up at the clouds that gather above the conflagration of Tinkers harboured below.

'It's St. Swithin's Day,' he says, 'You ever take the time to watch the sky, Julius? The way every billow spills against another, rising and colliding with the wonder of storms …but all pushed in the same direction by whichever wind prevails.'

Like the Tinkers, you mean.

'I wonder if they know they're late-evening clouds,' he says, '…drifting in the flames of a dying sun. No matter how they fight it gets closer to the horizon by the minute.'

Are we the wind of that change, Michael? Can we not hold ourselves above becoming the fatal Catalyst of Uniformity?

'I don't hold any more wish than you for the victory of Uniformity over Chaos, Julius, but I do have a need for the ease with which I can earn money. So tell me …where's *your* heart? Are you to be the cloud or the wind?'

I'm a weather front, I tell him, with smalls of clean washing flapping the line to show the wind's journey …and sometimes I'm the arrival of showering rain and want to run through the splash of streets shouting …'Take in your coffins …for I am ruinous to your Eternal Rest.'

'Then why don't you?'

The worms always beat me to it.

'They're slow,' says O'Daly, '…but most persistent.'

The boat is down now from the top of the van and the Fox is beside it with a yellow duster the Mammy showed her the instructions for.

The van door is opening …and inside …on a bolt of black velvet like a flare against the Eternal Night …is Jonjo Benigglety, late King of Tinkers.

I look away and the Mammy is watching me.

'Don't take this the wrong way,' she says, 'but I wouldn't be surprised if there wasn't still a smile on his face.'

The bucket of cold water was no use, then?

'Tigers swim,' she says, '…and eat Fish too when they can catch 'em …so don't be so *feck'n* obvious. He died laughing.'

And the cause of such frivolity?

'You,' she says, '…and how gullible you were to take on all his responsibility.'

He said that?

'He said no such thing,' she says, 'But we all know it.'

Did he mention me at all?

'Not the once,' she said, 'He looked up at me and mumbled then he was gone.'

What *did* he say?

'Strike Three.'

I am thumped awake by a Tinker the size of a small people-carrier who says, 'Shall we put him in now or wait until it's in the river?'

I look up at Dealy who's fixing the ropes from his roof rack. He looks away quickly.

Put him in now, I say, for if there comes a problem once you're in the water it might be too late.

A Tinker takes Dealy around to the front of his van to point out a small mark in the paintwork while they slide Jonjo onto a frame of wooden pallets and another siphons diesel from the tank for the fire.

The Tinkers scowl across at each other, all the while patting their pockets until one comes up with a matchbox. He shakes it open and there is just the one inside.

Here, I say, Use these.

I take the two tickets from my jacket and hold them out.

'Are you mad?' says O'Daly.

He catches hold of my arm but I gently release his fingers.

Never more so, I tell him, Have you ever been so mad it goes full circle?

He shakes his head in regret.

'Kayla tells me I'm yet only half-way around the bend.'

Sanity is not a Transient Condition, I say, It's a True State of Being. From within Sanity it's possible to do the maddest things. Things far more unimaginably mad than the merely insane could ever devise.

'I'll leave that to the Truly Deranged,' says O'Daly, 'The scent of Dementia can become overpowering. Are you sure you don't have the whiff of it yourself?'

The only scent in my nostrils, I say, is Freedom …and God, how clean that smells.

'It has a remarkable similarity to diesel in my own,' says O'Daly.

The Tinkers walk away with my two tickets. O'Daly and I stand to watch as they light them with the single match and walk around the boat setting fire to the fuel-soaked timber. Small flames sway and shimmer in the shadow cast by Jonjo's huge carcass.

'Why did you do that?' says O'Daly, 'You never know…'

Insanity is wasted on the insane, I tell him, Only the Truly Sane get to enjoy the experience.

'And are you now happy?' says O'Daly.

Madly, I tell him.

The Fox stands in front of me as the boat is slid into the dark river …Tinkers wade deep as armpits in the swirl of reeds …and her cheeks are aglisten with silent water.

I gently lower my hands onto her shoulders …and just as gently she shrugs me off.

'I'm not your Fox anymore, McEarly.'

She reaches up and her fingers nibble the blanket with which Ruby has wrapped our daughter against the river-chill air.

'I'm *her* Fox now,' she says.

…and there is a leaping of fire within the belly of the boat …and the Tinkers push it from the reeds into the centre of the stream where it finds us both adrift …and the fuel soaked to the timber takes and the pyre soars to envelop the singed remnant of sail that Dealy has fitted to the front. Before it goes I catch sight of a wavering advert for Taxis …the driver doffing a peaked cap to a shapely leg in seamed stocking escaping the door of his cab …and I wonder do I need to catch that number …but the stream swings it around and my last escape route goes up with the flame…

Beyond the diesel smoke that palls the river stands a silent figure in bright orange tweed.

'Did you ever see such a blaze?' says O'Daly.

Rarely, I say.

'And look at it go.'

…and listen to it come …the grass under my feet is leaping towards this forest fire and carrying me along with it…

'If this wasn't such a sad occasion,' says O'Daly, 'I would find it very sad.'

He turns to Dealy, 'A fine boat, Mr Dealy. A very fine boat. How they will love him when he reaches the Town.'

He won't get that far, I tell him, this is a Dealy special.

'He'll be stopped by the Weir at the Manor,' says Dealy.

'There's a lock there,' says O'Daly.

'He won't get past,' says Dealy, 'He hasn't the handle for the gate.'

I reach out for the door of the caravan as we pass.

The Fox stops me.

Ingvild?

'Not today.'

…the glisten is gone from her cheeks …wiped into the green sleeve of her jerkin but the eyes are bigger and more feral than I've ever seen…

'It's not ready,' she says.

Is it the Moon?

'No, McEarly, It's not the Moon. Nor your mincingly poetic way of describing it. Everyone knows she doesn't wear skirts.'

…and that foxes don't dance amongst her silver…?

'It's respect,' she says, 'They take time to get used to a new owner.'

The bus doors glower open at the Terminus …the frayed brushes at the bottom like lowered eyelashes as the Cortège troops silently on board. The driver stands in his little cab with cap in hand and a solemn nod to each one.

I usher the Ruby on board from behind and wait on the platform until everyone is seated. As I start to move he reaches out to catch my arm.

'That'll be one pound and twenty of the little ones.'

I thought Funerals travelled free, I say.

'Yes,' he says, '…they do. This is just for you.'

But I'm with them.

'It's only the Cortège travels free,' he says, 'I can hardly tell the Inspector that you're part of the Cortège. Your hair's the wrong colour for a start.'

But I'm related as of a week ago, I tell him.

'Everything is relative,' he says.

How long is it since you saw an Inspector?

'This very morning there was one in the Canteen,' he says.

Should he not have been out Inspecting?

'He's relatively static,' he says. He casts an eye over the Tinkers along the seats, '…not that anything stands still for long around here.'

Has he ever moved?

'Not noticeably,' he says, '…but every time I come back in he seems to have aged terribly.'

Back home the Mammy walks into the living room to see two empty couches by the window and breaks down in tears. Gudrun and Sigrid take a hold either side and guide her to the left one. She stares wistfully at the depression of broken springs left by Benigglety in the other.

'I shall miss his *oul* carcass,' she says, 'Only real gentleman I ever met …and that does include you, McEarly.'

Swimming Out Loud

'Julius,' says O'Daly, 'I've been asked to arrange another meeting between you and your man.'

I don't have a man, I tell him, a Ruby and a child …and once I had a Fox …with the occasional Mammy thrown in like a distress flare …but certainly no man.

'He wants you to come back to the Educational Fold', says O'Daly.

And who are you, I ask, his didactic sheepdog? Or is that a purely academic question?

'Not at all,' says O'Daly, 'I'm the Jack Russell that's going to *feck your leg* until you agree to meet him.'

The steps down to the Aquarium are wet with the rain that arrived in time to quench the final glow of Benigglety and has poured singularly ever since.

Under an umbrella at the bottom is the orange tweed of Professor Archibald Aloysius Montague. He flashes the air between us with slips of printed paper.

'I have the tickets, Julian.'

Julius …please.

'You know,' he says, 'I actually think I prefer your shortened version. Not much of a disguise though, was it.'

As a précis of War and Peace, I say, It'll do for now.

'And McCleary to McEarly was hardly the makings of an inspired intelligence.'

The one thing O'Daly always beats me to on the morning bus is the Anagram, I say, I can't see them …I think I'm not wired that way.

'So which one *are* you?' he says.

…and as we push through the doors into the humidity inside, I suggest that might be what we've come to discover…

'I'm all for the Discovery,' he says, 'Look here…'

He points out the progression of Informative Posters pinned to the wall for the schooling of small fish in uniforms.

'What is it you discovered in here, Juli …us.'

I tap the first poster…

Life, I say, in all its Inconceivable Diversity.

'And the second?'

That this is my Domain …along with all the Fish that Swim the Sea.

He rattles the third poster with the tip of his folded umbrella, 'And this one?'

I have repossessed my Kingdom, I say, The Power and the Glory will just as surely follow and since the birth of my daughter I am now forever and ever …amen.

'And Family?' he says.

I have one now, Monty, though as yet there is a degree of fragmentation with which I am not happy.

'What's your problem?' he says.

It's Benigglety, I say, your man has left behind a displacement that would take an Archimedes to quantify.

'Was he not the same Genus?' says Monty.

I tap the next poster.

Between 'Family' and 'Genus' comes 'Tribe'…and Tribe demands a sense of belonging …and that's where I find myself in question.

'Where's your heart in all this?'

Drifting with the wind, I tell him, and colliding with wonders...

'And when you found Life,' he says, '...how did that feel?'

I'd hidden from her so long she drenched me head to foot in Dichotomy as punishment.

'Not a pretty colour,' he says, '...and not one that suits you.'

Better than the sackcloth and ashes of dishonesty.

'You were never dishonest,' he says, 'Just afraid of being so. It's the world that's dishonest, Julius. Not you.'

He walks up and down the gaudy array of posters and I ask what he's looking for.

'The one that has 'Hypocrisy' in big letters,' he says, 'Though I've come to learn it's only ever spoken of in lower case these days.'

Even in Educated Circles?

'The very Tap Root.'

He takes my arm to lead me through the tanks, 'Come on, Julius. Take me to the Shoal. The need for a Damascene moment is about to descend upon my soul.'

From the counter of the café I watch as he approaches the tank. He stops three feet away and I wait ...he moves closer ...I refuse milk and sugar ...he moves closer ...steam blasts from petrified 'o' rings and clouds the air between us ...he moves closer ...cups rattle into saucers ...his nose is to the glass ...the eyes beyond it congregate towards him ...I hand over money for the coffee ...I watch ...a woman beside me pushes my tray aside with hers ...I wait ...I ignore the voices demanding that I move and then ...there it is ...the movement that starts within the tweed ...barely discernible to the uninitiated eye ...but there it is...

I slide the tray onto the table and walk over to put my hand on his shoulder. The tweed holds water from the rain that escaped the folding umbrella as we came in and is rough under my hands as if it's been frayed through rocky stream-beds and a thousand fronds of reed.

Monty? I say.

The movement accelerates under my hand and suddenly he's swimming out loud …and suddenly …we're both swimming out loud…

'Julius,' he says. He places his hands against the glass. His fingers spread until the webs between are the most obvious things in space, 'I'm swimming.'

Coffee, I say.

'Coffee, Julius?'

I pull him away from the glass and steer him to the table.

Even the biggest fish need coffee, I tell him.

He reaches over to pour salt in his cup. I let it pass. His hard palette bone will sense the edge of the cup and his scales will bristle and repair themselves at the bitterness of it.

'Thank you, Julius,' he says, 'I never …never …'

His hand is shaking …the cup is a rattling white against the spills in the saucer …I touch his hand …the skin is splashed with coffee he can't feel…

We're all Fish, I tell him, The only difference is that some of us inhabit smaller ponds than others.

'But I was swept, Julian …swept …there was a tide and I swam with it …all I had to do was steer…'

He rises quickly with arms spanned like fins and a passing tray clatters to the floor. Coffee peppers his trousers with burnt umber stains …voices raise and shriek …and in the midst of it all he gyrates …arms outstretched …rising and falling on a secret, invisible wave.

Slowly he takes the chair again and his hands fall to his sides.

'Where have I been until now, Julius?' he says.

His eyes are deepest black and the salt sea spills from them across his face.

On the outside, I tell him, but barely a step away.

'I don't want to be outside, Julius,' he says, '...and not until now did I know that.'

You needed to be, I tell him, In order to do what you've done with your life.

'But where did that step take me, Julius?'

To become another Brick in the Wall, I say, while here in the Shoal all fish are born equal and individual ...they choose whether or not to follow a tide. Most do out of a sense of family ...like the Tinkers ...and there is a great comfort can be derived from that ...but if they don't like the tide they find themselves in they are free to swim off to find another.

'I came to bring you back, Julius. But now I understand why you might not want to.'

Welcome to The Shoal, I say.

'What will you do there?' he says.

I'll be an honest man and live in poverty with the Ruby.

The mops have cleaned and gone away and we're allowed to regain our seats. Monty has paid for another tray of drinks all round and apologetic smiles and nods have become the fashion.

Through the open doors the Shoal is watching. I don't tell him ...but they are smiling too.

'Julius,' he says, 'What is it you think you did that frightened you so?'

The codlings are a-flutter in the corner of the tank and their cooled adrenalin reaches out to give me the support I need...

I take a deep breath...

I calculated the winning numbers for the Lottery, I tell him.

'Show me how you did it,' he says.

I would but Ingvild has kept the papers.

'Ingvild?'

The Fox.

'In words of one syllable, Julius, just what was it you did?'

I created a Formula, I tell him, which encompassed all the trending available since the inception of the Lottery.

'Does the Universe allow you to ignore the Laws of Probability?'

You'd have to ask Mrs Dealy.

'Where did you find the sheer computing power to run a program the size of that?'

I hacked the Universities Worldwide Intranet.

'How would you get away with that?'

By inserting a small innocuous programme into each one's daily routine, I tell him, Then I linked them so that as each one made a significant progression towards its own conclusion, it shared that data around the others, forcing them to make a constant reassessment of their own findings.

'Wouldn't that produce a chaotic result?'

If you stand far enough back from Chaos, Monty, as I'm sure you remember, you begin to see the pattern emerging.

'And what did you get?'

Seven Numbers, I tell him.

'And how many tickets did you buy to test this Theory, Julius?'

Ten, I say, so I could dilute the dishonesty by a significant proportion should my calculation be correct.

'And did it turn out to be any more than a Theory?'

This was the first of Life's Dichotomies, I say, for it appears I ran the last pages of the calculation backwards. It should have been wrong but it wasn't.

'Does your Formula allow for that?' he says, 'You found a way to manage the Universal Inconstant?'

I bought nine tickets with my numbers on ...and as a 'Control Element' I had a Lucky Dip.

'That should pave the way to Extinction for any Theory. What happened?'

The Asteroid of Life's Dichotomies, I tell him, for the Lucky Dip had the same numbers.

'Didn't that tell you something, Julian?'

'Yes …It told me to get out of there quickly before I was besieged.

'I saw what you did at the funeral,' he says, 'What did you do with the other eight tickets?'

I gave them to strangers on the railway station. Someone should reap the benefits of advanced mathematics. It's a long-overdue natural progression.

'So why not you?' he says, 'Are you no less deserving? What did the Ruby say about it?'

I haven't told her. She thinks I'm fool enough without trying to explain the life I've turned her away from.

'It's not too late,' says Monty, 'You could try again.'

I couldn't do with the dishonesty, I tell him, I went to the shop counter where I'd bought the tickets then turned and walked away with just my spare pair of shoes and two shirts in a carrier. I haven't been back since.

'And if you'd made it to the counter, what then?'

I wouldn't have been me.

Monty stares across the table at me …his eyes slowly dissolving to brown as Life filters back in …a dark humour flowing around his lips.

'And who *are* you?' he says.

…and I have no idea…

Tell me, I say.

'I will, he says, 'You're the man who ran away on the week the Lottery broke down and gave everyone the same numbers.'

And the little balls?

'All balls…' he says.

And the randomisation?

'Now there's the *real* Asteroid strike,' he says, 'Either the Infinite Monkeys in their Infinite Cage are due to conclude their rewriting of the Works of Shakespeare at any minute, or you, my friend, are the Unwitting Victim of Lady Coincidence.'

She made a Monkey of me?

'Infinitely.' says Monty.

Then I have a new apprentice for you, I tell him.

The Colour Diesel

The caravan is dark inside. I wade through the carpet until I have the curtains drawn and the windows pushed wide. I turn around in amazement for it seems as though professionals have fixed the furniture. Everything sparkles in the meadow-light streaming the windows and the upholstery is plumped proud and dust-free.

'Cnut and Ragnar,' says Shel, 'They're thinking of looking for a job.'

…I am dumb with admiration for the workmanship…

I have the very place, I say.

The foreman folds up the paper as I walk into the cabin.

'McEarly,' he says, 'So good of you to join us. To what do we owe this honour?'

I'm leaving, I tell him.

'I thought that was three weeks ago,' he says, 'I'm sat only now waiting for the Notice to come in.'

I'm sorry, I say, I should have called earlier.

'Take a look outside,' he says.

I poke my head out of the door to see Dealy walking around in the loose chippings over by the spilled gluepot. He gets taller by the minute as I watch. Under the shed awning are the faint outlines of three coffins.

Are those the same…

'The same three,' he says.

What's he been doing?

'I can't catch up with him,' he says, 'Only three weeks ago the Garda swore they seen a Viking Longboat leave the yard and I tell them the river's a three mile hike and that's a long way on tarmac with just oars and a small sail.'

I came to talk to you about this, I say.

...I slide the watch from my wrist and push it across the table...

'It's a watch,' he says.

Did nobody think to look closely at it?

'Aye, McEarly, I had to,' he says, 'For it has the three hands and no Mickey Mouse to say which is which.'

Did you never think to read the name on it?

'Them things are all over from the China,' he says.

Not this one...

He squints at it upside down on the table.

'You mean,' he says, 'It's a *real* xeloR?'

A real one, I say.

'To think,' he says, 'I had a ten pound watch in my hand all them times.'

You can have it on extended loan, I say, on two conditions...

He hears me out...

'I'll think about it,' he says.

Then I'll hold the watch while you do.

He pulls back the watch...

'I thought about it,' he says.

The Ruby helps the Mammy downstairs and into the sitting room. The Mammy shakes her head at the empty couch previously occupied by the huge presence that was Jonjo Benigglety.

'I can't get over it,' she says, 'It's five weeks and every morning I expect him to still be there. I mean ...I hope.'

…and the tears shed willingly …and their tails flick clean lines through the hasty make-up she's put on …just in case…

'Mammy …Mammy,' says the Ruby.

'It's no good, Ruby,' says the Mammy, 'I'm going to have to move.'

The Ruby looks at me …and all the while biting her lip.

'Julius…' she says.

…and I find it strange that anyone with a bereft Mammy should want to attach them to a loose cannon that might have carelessly lost their very own…

She can have my flat, I say.

'Is that the best you can do, McEarly?' says the Mammy …and the tears boil away from her cheeks… 'What about the *feck'n* stairs?'

There are no stairs in a flat, I tell her, that's why it's called…

'There's the two flights to the outside,' she says, 'So it's no good and that's an end to it.'

There's a tug at my sleeve that I had lately been too busy to notice the absence of …and now the sensation of the nibbling fills my heart with a burning desire to turn back the clock…

'Look,' says the Fox, 'This bit slides across like this.' She tugs a strip of chromium and a partition twists an elegant step to become a wall. 'Then you pull it around the corner …like this.'

And a door appears as if from nowhere and behind it is a room of unbelievable capacity. I look in…

It has a bed and everything.

'The one I was born in, remember,' says the Fox, 'And the same one my Mammy…'

I think you paid that back, I tell her.

'I hope so, McEarly,' she says.

Two for the price of one, I say, Better than the Co-op.

'Then why did you try to stop me, McEarly?' says the Fox.

Look at yourself, I say, There's more meat on a strip light. There isn't the three pints inside you at all.

'That's why it took four days,' says the Fox, 'A bit at a time is better than a drenching.'

Tell that to Lady Life, I say, and while you have her distracted, see if you can steal her bucket.

'McEarly,' she says, 'Watch this…'

…and she walks around the caravan drawing out walls and partitions until the whole is sectioned and separated…

Is this how you lived?

'No,' she says wistfully, '…but we could've.'

Then why didn't you?

'The Heap was warmer in winter,' she says, 'But now I have the chance, I'll show you how to manage a house.'

Caravan, I say, and anyway you're going to University. Monty will take you like a shot.

'An hour with me and he'd wish he had been,' she says, 'I lack Formality, in case you hadn't noticed.'

Monty's one of the good guys. Don't turn him down out of hand.

'You ever hear of Distance Learning, McEarly?'

Sure, I say, It's a growing pastime.

'Well,' says the Fox, 'The bigger the distance, the better I learn. Besides …I have my own tutor.'

…teeth nibble my sleeve and my face begins to fold into smile lines…

'Don't get carried away, McEarly,' she says, 'I'm just reminding you of your responsibilities.'

Outside the caravan the air is sweet with possibilities of grass and riverbanks and the stark white of daisies flooding the water meadow …and where the sun strikes the tiny buttercupped bees they sing to the wind like the string section of Nature's Frantic Orchestra.

Who cleaned up the field? I ask.

'We think it was Loki,' says the Fox.

'I am not travelling in that *Feck'n Contraption.*' says the Mammy.

It was Jonjo's, I remind her.

'Alright then,' she says, 'But where are we going?'

Home.

'I'm not having this *feck'n contraption* on my bus again,' says the driver, 'What is it you're trying to work here, McEarly.'

He shuffles around in his little cab to squint closely at the Mammy. She bats him away with the handbag.

'I heard about Dealy with the pigs,' he says, 'You have some kind of scam going now with the Elderly? Is there a profit in the smuggling?'

No, I tell him, for you only get one of these to a coffin.

'I'm not staying here,' says the Mammy.

Why not?

'Everybody will think I'm a Tinker.'

And?

'Alright, McEarly,' she says, 'So I *am* a Tinker, but what makes you think I want everyone else to know?'

I take the woolly bonnet off the head of the granddaughter cradled in her arms.

Not *my* Genes, I tell her.

'They bypassed you like everything else, McEarly,' says the Mammy, 'Have you settled on a name for her yet?'

Joanne Josephine, I say.

The Mammy thinks a moment…

'Aha,' she says, 'Joan-Jo…'

…and the child disappears somewhere in an amplitude of bosoms and black wool cardigan until barely a glimpse of her flame remains …and tears flow down a cleanly-washed face leaving no scars in a world once more replete…

'Julius?' says the Ruby, 'What shall we do with all this space?'

I don't know, I say, Populate it?

'That might take a few years,' she says, 'but what until then?'

What about a Tribe of Ikeans?

'They want to stay in the house,' she says, 'Cnut and Ragnar are at the timberyard. Gudrun and Sigrid have their Cleaning Service for the Elderly going at a real pace. It's much easier for them to be there what with the bus stop by the door.'

Where's Loki?

'We're never sure,' she says.

'Michael,' says Kayla Shaughnessy, 'There's more space in this one room than in your whole flat.'

O'Daly studies my face from the doorway.

'I'm not sure,' he says, 'Motives being what they may be…'

I swear, I say.

'On what?' he says.

On the Repatriated Soul of a One Kilo Chicken.

'That would about do it,' he says.

'McEarly,' says the Mammy, 'This meadow is a wonderful place for the young …but if like me you're approaching middle-age …the morning mist from the river plays havoc with your joints.'

'We don't *have* to stay here…'

…it's the Fox …beside me and nibbling the sleeve with one hand and the blanket with the other and all the while making sure I don't say something that might reverberate within me for ever…

'We can move the caravan,' she says.

How do we do that?

'It has wheels,' she says.

And are there enough of us stented and able to push?

'We have a truck,' says the Fox.

Have you seen it lately? I say, For there's grass where the wheels should be showing and the last time it moved it was the spiders picked it up and lifted it into the shade.

'It runs,' she says, 'All it needs is for you to clean it.'

How do you know it runs?

'I fixed it,' she says, 'Once O'Daly agreed to take over my shifts I had the spare time. So I fixed it.'

But I don't know how to drive.

'I do,' says the Fox.

You can't, I say, you're not yet thirteen.

'Licences are an Optional Extra for Tinkers.'

And the Insurance?

'Against what? Who do you think is going to argue with a whole family of Tinkers?'

I'm not a Tinker, I tell her.

'Don't kid yourself,' she says, 'The Adoption Papers came through last week.'

I've adopted you?

'No,' she says, 'Try the other way around…'

'I can drive,' says Kayla, '…if Ingvild will show me how the truck works.'

Kayla backs up the truck until Ingvild can clip the tow bar to it. As I stow away the gas and generator an Astra van trundles slowly across the meadow.

'I thought I'd wish you on your way, Mr McEarly.'

…it's Dealy of the outstretched hand of friendship …now that I'm leaving…

'Since you've been gone I'm allowed in the cabin,' he says, 'I knew all along it was your lighter my bushel was hiding under.'

Dealy, I tell him, You're the Wisest Virgin I ever met.

I take his hand.

…and deep inside me is a perverse pocket in which he and his wisdom will reside wherever I go…

The cat? I say.

'I got a new one,' he says, 'A Rescue Cat. I saved it from the Indian around the corner.'

Is it chipped?

'Have you learned nothing in all this time, Mr McEarly?'

'Get in, Julius,'

Kayla is taking instruction from the Fox on the fact that the gear lever has been assembled back to front.

'It's easier to reach when you're small,' she says.

Between them they find a suitable ratio and we lurch the wheels from the troughs they've made in the soil of the meadow. By the time we get to the gate a young man is standing by, holding it open. There is a familiarity about his handsomely mischievous face that I can't quite place.

'Thanks, Loki,' says the Fox as we pass through. I catch a glance through the mirror outside the door but he has disappeared.

What's this little dial do?

I tap the circular glass lens and the needle shakes it's way further to the bottom.

'It's the diesel gauge,' says the Fox.

Why is it red? Is that the colour of it?

'No,' she says, 'That's the colour of money.'

I'd forgotten, I say, It's been a while.

Kayla draws us onto the filling station forecourt.

'Somebody had better remember it pretty quickly,' she says, 'There's only enough for about another five miles.'

O'Daly, Ruby, the Mammy and Joan-Jo are comfortable in the wide back seat of the cab. Blank looks shine all around.

The Fox shrugs in a way I haven't seen since the day in the park when all the weight of her world descended on those fragile shoulders.

'Look in the glove box, McEarly.'

What's one of those, I say, I never had but the one glove and surely I wouldn't need a box to put that in.

She reaches over and pops open a section of the dashboard. I look but there's no money in there either. She reaches in and pulls out a screwdriver.

Oh no, I tell her, we're not beginning this journey by screwing the meter.

'Come with me,' she says, and leaps from the cab.

I follow her around to the door of the caravan.

'Hold the door open,' she says.

…and in her hand the screwdriver is a twinkle as she extracts the screws from the threshold strip that stops the carpet from washing out of the door…

She holds up the piece of aluminium.

They won't take that, I say, there's no weight in the metal. You wouldn't get more than fifty pence…

'McEarly,' she says, 'You're babbling. Just hold it.'

…and she peels back the carpet …and the underlay beneath is an inch and a half thick multitude of colours …mainly brown, blue and red…

Is that *Money*?

'What does it look like, McEarly?'

It looks like a Money Carpet. Is it fitted?

'Wall to Wall,' she says.

Whose is it?

'Yours,' says the Fox, 'Remember? …the caarrvaan …an effertin innit?'

Oh Jonjo, I say, No wonder you died laughing.

'He gave you everything you ever ran away from,' she says, '…and now you have it, would you give it up?'

And disgrace his memory?

Kayla crunches gears and jerks us out onto the main road. She straightens up and looks for somewhere to park.

'Anywhere,' says the Fox, 'You're a Tinker now.'

Kayla turns in the seat, 'Anyone have an idea where we're going?'

'Does it matter,' says O'Daly, '…as long as there are Shoals aplenty and Chickens to Repatriate?'

'Then I'll take sensible suggestions,' she says.

I have an idea.

'I'm almost afraid to ask,' says Kayla.

Shel, I say, Click your heels.

'McEarly,' says the Fox, 'You …Are …So …So …Dead.'

www.ingramcontent.com/pod-product-compliance
Lightning Source LLC
Chambersburg PA
CBHW070001120726
47909CB00003B/767